SHAMEFUL SECRET, SHOTGUN WEDDING

BY
SHARON KENDRICK

First published in Great Britain 2010
Harlequin Mills & Boon Limited,
Eton House, 18-24 Paradise Road, Richmond, Surrey TW9 1SR

© Sharon Kendrick 2010

ISBN: 978 0 263 87844 8

Harlequin Mills & Boon policy is to use papers that are natural,
renewable and recyclable products and made from wood grown in
sustainable forests. The logging and manufacturing process conform
to the legal environmental regulations of the country of origin.

Printed and bound in Spain
by Litografia Rosés, S.A., Barcelona

SHAMEFUL SECRET, SHOTGUN WEDDING

**This book is dedicated to the Hempstock family—
with whom I used to spend many happy times
in Dronfield as a child.**

CHAPTER ONE

THERE was something about him which made her think of danger. Something dark and tantalising which drew her gaze like a magnet. Cassie felt the rush of blood to her cheeks and the sudden pounding of her heart as she stared at the man across the busy holiday rush of the department store.

He was *gorgeous*. Too gorgeous to be real, surely? Why, if she hadn't been surrounded by tinsel, fairy lights and a packed working schedule until the big day itself she might have thought that Christmas had come early.

Not that she had a lot to compare him with. It was only the second time she'd been away from rural Cornwall—where most of the men she met wore cheap aftershave and trod on your toes while you were dancing. And when you got up close for the slow numbers you could see little pieces of blood-stained tissue paper on their chins, where they'd cut themselves shaving.

Which was why landing this temporary job in London's most glitzy department store over the festive season was Cassie's chance to get away from the predictable world she'd grown up in and to live the dream. And London at this time of the year *was* a dream—an enchanted world of fairy lights and fake snow and an air of expectation. She *loved* Christmas.

Even working on the 'Seasonal Candle' section—a fir-festooned grotto selling a variety of upmarket candles—was a dream. One which remained intact despite the best efforts of mealy-mouthed Lindy in nearby Cosmetics and the fact ten hours of standing made your feet scream with protest. Daily, Cassie dealt with stick-thin society matrons and laughing students and over-excited small children filing past her on their way to see Santa.

Only today, she could see someone rather different from her usual customer—a tall, brooding man with skin the colour of burnished olive. Clad in a dark cashmere overcoat, his face proud and aristocratic, his lips mock-ingly sensual—and yet there was a cold, hard glint to his eyes of pure ebony.

Cassie's heart started racing. Racing hard enough to burst. She was certain he wasn't interested in buying a candle—in fact, she was surprised to see him shopping at all. He looked like the sort of man who would have minions to do the more mundane chores in life and one who would *never* cut himself shaving. She didn't imagine he'd be tempted by her sales pitch, either—but something made her walk up to him, her bright professional smile fixed firmly in place.

Never in her life had Cassie been so conscious of anyone's presence. He seemed to own the space around him simply by existing in it and exuded a rare kind of charisma which made people stop and take a second look.

Suddenly dizzy and wondering what insane instinct had propelled her into his vicinity, she drew a deep breath. 'Good afternoon, sir—I wonder can I interest you in one of these beautiful candles?'

Giancarlo's brows knitted together as a banal little sentence interrupted his reverie and he found himself staring into a pair of violet eyes of extraordinary beauty. He was used to the adulation of women in general and salesgirls were no exception—and he really wasn't in the mood to be engaging. But he *was* supposed to be buying Christmas gifts for all his admin staff and the girl who was trying to sell him something *was* very pretty—so he gave her his attention. 'A candle?' he drawled.

Cassie nodded. His sexy Italian accent matched his Mediterranean looks, adding yet another layer to his allure—and silently she despaired at her own stupidity.

She might not have a wealth of experience about the opposite sex but she was intuitive enough to recognise when a man was completely out of her league. And this one most definitely was. Why, his clothes just screamed class and quality and his demeanour was more than impressive—it was daunting. So don't just stand there gawping at him like a stranded fish—*say something*!

'That's right, sir. But not just *any* candle—this is the biggest selection you'll find in London. Irresistible specialities for the festive season.' Cassie widened her smile and wondered whether his face was always so dark and so forbidding. 'It *is* Christmas. Or hadn't you noticed?'

Giancarlo gave a shrug. It wasn't his favourite time of year, no—but on closer inspection his attention was captured by more than the seasonal mayhem going on around him. Because she was exquisite. Absolutely *exquisite*. With skin like quietly gleaming satin and hair like silk. And a body which should have carried a health warning—even though she was wearing the rather plain store uniform. Through the faint miasma produced by jet lag and overwork, he felt the sudden prickling of his senses.

'Christmas?' he murmured. 'Would that have anything to do with the choir of angels I'm hearing—or is that the effect you have on all your customers?' He saw the colour rise in her cheeks and gave a lazy smile. 'Look, why don't you tell me what it is you're selling and we shall see if you can persuade me to buy?'

Cassie nodded. Trying to ignore the now frantic crashing of her heart, she drew an arc with her hand in front of the glittering display as she slipped smoothly into the script of her sales patter. 'Well, these candles all come in a wide range of scents. The Christmas Chocolate has proved to be one of our most popular varieties this year. It's dark and spicy—with subtle undertones of mulled wine.'

'And is that your favourite?'

'My…my *favourite*?'

'Mmm. Surely you must have a favourite?'

For a second, her sales pitch deserted her. She hadn't been asked that before. And when *he* asked it, he made her feel special. Different. Oh, but she was an idiot! But she still looked into the gleam of his black eyes and answered as honestly as she could. 'To be honest, I like this one best. It smells of sweet oranges. And cloves. Sort of…traditional. And nostalgic. Everybody loves them. All ages. They have universal appeal. Especially at this time of year.'

There was a pause and Giancarlo felt another quick beat of desire as he heard the wistful little note in her voice. 'You've got a deal,' he said softly. 'I'll take half a dozen.'

Cassie opened her eyes wide. 'You mean *six*?' she squeaked.

'Unless the definition of half a dozen has changed since the last time I heard it?' he questioned gravely.

'N-no. Certainly, sir. Six it is.'

While she was wrapping them—with fumbling fingers which seemed much less dextrous than usual—he asked her a series of questions, and in view of the commission she was going to make on the sale, it seemed rude not to answer them. No, she didn't live in London, she was only here for the holiday season, and no, she wasn't wearing coloured contact lenses—her eyes really *were* that colour. But in truth, his presence was so distracting that she could barely think straight.

Giancarlo watched as she snipped the end of a claret-coloured ribbon and tugged at the finished bow with a flourish. She was just too good to walk away from, he decided—with that pale blonde hair and violet eyes and a body shaped like a bottle of Verdicchio.

He'd spent most of the past month in New York—labouring away on a tough deal he'd only just pulled off by the skin of his teeth. One of those deals which had seen him still at his desk at midnight and beyond. His name had been splashed all over the financial papers, he'd stacked up a few million dollars—and then quietly siphoned off a substantial portion to a cause far more worthy than his already bloated bank account. All in all, it had been a successful trip—just like the one before, and the one before that. But success could be draining—sometimes it took you away from the fundamentals in life. And he was sick of the relentless march of Christmas with its in-your-face commercialism and over-the-top celebration.

What he needed was a little light relaxation with a female of the species. And not some ball-breaking woman who liked to work and play as hard as a man and gave you a lecture on equality if you so much as opened a door for her. Until you made the mistake of taking her away for a long weekend—when suddenly she was talking three-carat diamond rings and church weddings.

No. He wanted someone soft and unchallenging. Someone easy on the eye and easy on the mind. Someone who would massage his ego and a lot more besides. Like this sassy little thing with her soft, curving breasts and her peachy little bottom. He couldn't imagine *her* wanting to talk stocks and shares with him—or angling for a winter break in Hawaii!

'What time do you finish work?' he questioned as she took his credit card from him.

Cassie hesitated. 'Six-thirty,' she said, feeling on rather shaky territory here—but surely it would be rude not to answer a customer when he asked you a direct question?

'And you'll be going out for dinner afterwards?'

Cassie thought of the pan full of pasta and pesto which was sitting on the fat-spattered cooker back at the shared apartment which was currently her temporary home. As accommodation went it was pretty basic, but she was grateful to her old school-friend, Gavin, for letting her stay—even if it meant sleeping in a room which was little more than a cupboard.

'Well, sort of,' she prevaricated.

'Sort of?'

'I told my flatmates I'd have dinner with them.'

'And what if I asked you to have dinner with me instead?'

'I can't,' she breathed.

'Why not?'

She stared into his narrowed black eyes and her stomach gave a funny little lurch. 'Because I don't...I don't even *know* you.'

'So why don't I introduce myself and we'll get that problem out of the way?'

A hand was extended, and with proprietary ease, it captured hers. Cassie's hand had been shaken many times in her life—often by departing guests at the little B&B run by her mother. Or when she'd won a prize for ice-dancing, which was something she was particularly good at.

But never had it felt quite like this before....

His big hand made hers seem so tiny—and the warm touch of his bare skin against hers seemed, well...*intimate*, really. Or was that because his thumb brushed almost negligently against her palm—a movement so brief that she might almost have imagined it? Except the responding shiver of her skin told her she hadn't imagined anything.

'My name is Giancarlo Andrea Vellutini,' he said softly. 'I am Tuscan by birth and global by nature. What else would you like to know? That I have a house in London and my diary is empty tonight? I was planning to catch up on a stack of paperwork, but you...' he leaned forward and read her name badge '...Cassandra Summers...have tempted me into changing my plans.'

Cassie couldn't deny being tempted, too—and not just because the way he said her name made it sound like pure poetry. Invitations to dinner were pretty thin on the ground—and nobody remotely like this man Giancarlo had ever asked her out before. In fact, the most recent date she'd been on had consisted of someone from the computer department who'd taken her for a disgusting burger in a fast-food chain—and then claimed to have forgotten his wallet!

Yet instinct warned her against accepting this far more tantalising offer. That same deep instinct which had alerted her senses when she'd first set eyes on him. The one which told her that this man was dangerous—and not for the likes of her. He was too good-looking. Too urbane. Too rich. Too *everything*. And wasn't it more than a little arrogant of him to assume that she would drop everything and fit in with him just because he had decided he would change his plans?

'It's very sweet of you, but I'm afraid I can't let my flatmates down,' she said apologetically.

Giancarlo's eyes narrowed. The little shop-girl was turning him down? Inconceivable! 'You have a boyfriend?' he questioned curiously. 'Someone waiting at home for you?'

'No,' she said. 'There's no one. But my flatmates are relying on me to bring half their supper home from the delicatessen here.'

He wondered if she was playing games with him. Perhaps imagining that she would make herself more desirable by playing hard to get. Or was it possible that here was a woman who wasn't his for the taking—a woman with enough self-respect to say no? His lips curved into a thoughtful smile. Doubtful.

Pulling a thick cream business card from his wallet, he slid it between her unresisting fingers. 'Well, why don't you call me if you change your mind?'

She met his eyes, again feeling the unmistakable tingle of her skin where he'd touched her and wondering if he could feel it, too. She swallowed, plucking up every bit of courage she had. 'Or perhaps you could always come in another day?'

Dark eyebrows were elevated. 'And ask you again?'

'Well, yes.'

She thought he was about to start haunting the department store like some lovelorn young suitor? 'I don't think so,' he said silkily. *'Ciao, bella.'*

And to Cassie's consternation, he turned on his heel and walked away—just like that. For a moment she stood there watching the tall, striking figure in the cashmere coat until he had disappeared—and began to wonder if she had imagined the entire interlude. And then she looked down at the neatly wrapped package which was still sitting next to the till and realised that he had forgotten to take his candles and that it was too late to run after him.

All the way home on the bus, with the brightly wrapped candles lying on her lap, Cassie could have kicked herself. How *stupid* could she have been? Batting his invitation away as if men like him were queuing round the block to date her. How many times in life did an opportunity like that present itself—a gorgeous man offering to sweep you off your feet?

Her father's prolonged illness had been heartbreaking and she had been longing to get away from Cornwall. But hadn't she also come to London partly because she felt her life was passing her by and she wanted a little adventure? And surely it would be difficult to imagine a greater adventure than some tantalising Tuscan asking her to have dinner with him.

Still, at least she could comfort herself with the thought that she was a loyal friend and flatmate—and that she hadn't let the others down. Until she let herself into the apartment to find that the flat was empty and all the pasta had been eaten. Gavin had left her a note saying they'd all got too hungry to wait and had gone to the pub—and would she care to join them?

Well, what else was she going to do—scrub around in an empty fridge, trying to find something on the TV which wasn't a game show and trying not to think about what she *could* have been doing? An image of Giancarlo's mocking eyes swam into her memory as, with a frustrated little yelp, she slung the salad and the garlic bread into the empty fridge and went to change.

Wearing a pair of jeans and a warm coat over her sweater, Cassie walked through the cold night air to the pub. Her footsteps rang out on the icy pavement and bright stars spangled the clear skies. Even from the end of the road she could hear the noise and the bustle and when she opened the door of the pub, she was hit by a solid wall of sound.

Every inch of the place was packed. Beneath a swirl of paper streamers, people were swaying and singing along to a song about wishing it could be Christmas every day—which had been played every year since Cassie could remember. And, given the current decibel level and crush of bodies, it was not a sentiment she currently agreed with.

The queue to get to the bar was five-deep and heaven only knew where Gavin and the others were. Could she face battling her way through the crowds to sit nursing a mediocre glass of warm white wine for the rest of the evening and shouting to make herself heard above the noise?

No, she could not. With a decisiveness which surprised her, she turned and walked out of the pub again—her feet taking her straight back to the flat while a preposterous idea grew in her mind.

Only, maybe it was not *so* preposterous at all. He had given her his phone number, hadn't he? Told her to call him—and she had a good reason to call him, even if you discounted the fact that he was the most exciting thing to ever happen to her.

Letting herself into the apartment with a fast-beating heart and grateful for the quietness, Cassie punched out his number with a trembling finger before she could change her mind. She could hear the phone ringing and ringing. Maybe he was one of those people who screened their calls and, since he didn't recognise the number, wasn't going to bother answering. She was just about to hang up when she heard a click—and then that distinctive velvety, accented voice sounded in her ear.

'*Pronto*. Giancarlo Vellutini.'

'Giancarlo?' She swallowed down her nerves. 'It's me…Cassie.'

'*Chi?*' There was a pause. 'Who?'

This was humiliating. He didn't remember. Of *course* he didn't remember. He'd spoken to her for about five minutes and given her his business card on a whim. Cassie would have hung up there and then if it hadn't been for the candles which were still sitting on the side, wrapped in glittery gold and claret paper. 'Cassandra Summers. I work at Hudson's department store. We met today—do you remember? You bought some—'

'*Sì, sì, senz'altro—scusi, scusi.*' His voice dipped

effortlessly into English. 'Cassandra Summers with the amazing eyes. How could I possibly forget?'

Cassie swallowed as nerves began to assail her. Don't back him into a corner. Show that you have a legitimate reason to ring him in case he's looking for an out. 'Actually, I'm ringing up because you forgot your candles?'

'Excuse me?'

'You bought six very expensive c-candles and you didn't take them with you.'

His long legs sprawling in front of him as he reclined in a squashy leather sofa, Giancarlo looked up at the huge canvas which dominated the wall above the blazing log fire, and gave a slow smile. 'So I did. And that's the only reason you're ringing me, is it?'

'Well, I…' Flustered now, Cassie didn't know how to respond. Did she tell him that maybe she'd been a bit too hasty in turning him down—and that dinner sounded wonderful—or would that make her sound like some sort of desperado?

'Or maybe you've changed your mind about having dinner with me?' he prompted silkily.

Just say yes…he isn't planning to kidnap you and send you to the ends of the earth. *Just say yes!* 'That would be very…nice,' said Cassie blandly.

Giancarlo gave a soft laugh. Nice wasn't what he had in mind. Nothing near 'nice', in fact. Something dark, erotic and horizontal was closer to the mark—he knew that and he suspected that deep down she knew that, too. Because nobody could deny the sparks which had flown between them today—sparks hot enough to make him act on impulse, to chat up the kind of woman he would never have met at a dinner party.

And yet, in a way, he had preferred her a little more when she'd lifted her chin and fixed him with those violet eyes and proudly said she was doing something else tonight. Wasn't it slightly disappointing that she'd rung and become just like all the others—joining the endless line of women who wanted him and didn't mind showing him how much? In a few short moments she'd gone from goddess to doormat and he'd known enough of those in his time. His mouth flattened. Wouldn't it have excited him if *he'd* had to do the chasing for once—instead of the inevitability of yet another luscious creature falling into his bed because he had snapped his fingers?

Still, he shouldn't knock it. At least, not until he'd tried it.

'So what time shall I expect you?' he murmured.

'*Expect* me?' Cassie squeaked. 'You mean have dinner with you *tonight*?'

'Of course. What did *you* mean? Unless you have eaten already?'

'Well, no—but it's…' Cassie glanced down at the bright pink waterproof watch which encircled her slender wrist. 'It's getting on for nine o'clock!'

'So?'

'Well, isn't that…?' Something stopped her from expounding her mother's theory that food lay heavy on your stomach if it was consumed too late in the evening. He didn't seem the kind of man who would be interested in that kind of information. 'A bit late to eat?'

'Not at all. In Spain, they eat at eleven.'

'I wouldn't know about that.'

'You've never been to Spain?'

'Never.'

'Then maybe I shall take you there one day,' he

murmured. 'We could drink Rioja under some of the starriest skies in the world and eat tapas with our fingers. But in the meantime—why don't you get in a cab and come over here and we'll see what we can find in my cupboard? Where do you live?'

'Greenford.'

'Near Park Lane?'

'No, no—that's Green Park,' she corrected, because it was a common mistake. As if she could ever afford to live anywhere near Park Lane! 'I'm miles out,' she forged on. 'Even with a fast car I couldn't possibly get there much before ten and—no matter what they do in Spain—that really is too late for dinner. Especially when I have to get up early for work tomorrow.'

It wasn't too late for what he had in mind but even Giancarlo wouldn't dream of issuing such a blatant invitation unless he had a woman in his arms and was kissing her into dreamy submission. He stifled a sigh—because this now seemed to be escalating into something other than an impromptu dinner with the inevitable conclusion he'd had in mind. The last thing he wanted was hassle. He didn't do hassle—and certainly not from women. Maybe it wasn't meant to happen after all.

'That's a pity,' he murmured.

Cassie could hear the dismissive note in his voice bringing the conversation to an end—and all she could think of was that her chance to see him was slipping away. And that she would never meet a man like Giancarlo Vellutini again.

'But I'm free tomorrow night,' she blurted out.

Giancarlo stared up at the ceiling, wondering why nothing was ever perfect, for now she sounded a little *too* keen. Should he tell her he was busy? It wasn't really a fabrication since he was *always* busy—and there was enough paperwork left over from the American deal to keep him occupied for days.

And then he thought of her face. Of her rose-petal lips and those eyes—the most vivid, violet colour he'd ever seen. In fact, come to think of it, he'd *never* seen a pair of eyes like that. He found himself thinking beyond her face. Wondering what kind of panties she favoured. And what she liked best to do in bed. And he swallowed down the sharp tang of lust which had dried in his throat.

'Then we must have dinner tomorrow,' he said unevenly. 'I'll send a car to collect you. What time do you finish at the store?'

'I...' Cassie's thoughts began rattling through her head as she tried to work out the logistics. She could take an outfit into work and get changed afterwards. 'That would be great. Tomorrow I finish at seven-thirty.'

'The car will be waiting for you. *A domani*,' he said softly, and hung up.

Cassie was left listening to the click as he cut the connection, her heart racing as she replaced the phone in its cradle. She thought of the sensual curve of his lips and way his hard black eyes had glittered when he looked at her. She remembered the way her body had trembled when his hand had brushed over hers and she had the strangest sensation of standing beside a deep, dark lake and getting ready to dive in without really knowing anything about what might lay beneath the surface.

The only thing she knew was that she was going to be way out of her depth.

CHAPTER TWO

THERE must have been some kind of mistake.

For a moment Cassie froze as she stared up at the imposing white mansion. Yes, she'd guessed that Giancarlo was rich—very, very rich—but surely he couldn't live somewhere like *this*? Not looking out over the lush gardens of Kensington Palace and slap bang next door to an embassy where a flag was fluttering in the cold December breeze.

Already the evening felt as if it were happening to someone else—and yet it had barely begun. She kept thinking that if she pinched herself hard enough she might wake up and find herself on the bus going home to Greenford instead of in the back of a chauffeur-driven car which had just stopped in front of one of the most prestigious crescents in London.

After finishing work, she had changed into a simple black dress and a pair of cheap, high-heeled shoes that she'd hastily run out and bought during her lunch hour. Adding a touch of lipstick, she had untied her hair and tried to quell her steadily rising nerves as she dragged a brush through it. It was only when it was hanging loose in a pale waterfall down her back that Lindy from the cosmetics department had walked in, to see Cassie looking at herself in the mirror.

'Going somewhere?'

'Um, out for dinner.'

'Got a date?'

'Yes. Yes, I have.' She was dying to tell someone but she'd been asleep by the time her flatmates had arrived home last night—and Lindy had never been friendly towards her. Plus Lindy was a full-time member of staff—not someone who'd been drafted in for the Christmas period—and perhaps it wasn't really appropriate to tell her that she was dating a customer. Not when the expression on her face as she looked Cassie up and down was as sour as a bowlful of lemons.

Instead, Cassie glanced at her watch. 'Gosh, is that the time? I'd better go or I'll be late. See you tomorrow, Lindy.' Carefully, she picked up the distinctive claret-and-gold-wrapped package and smiled.

Lindy's sharp eyes narrowed. 'What's that?'

'Oh, just—just some candles. They belong to a... friend.' Did she know Giancarlo well enough to call him a friend—and why was she blushing? Why hadn't she just come out and said that a customer had left them behind? 'He asked me to bring them over.'

Lindy's eyebrows shot up. 'Did he?'

'Yes. Well, I'd better...I'd better go. Night, Lindy.'

Feeling ridiculously guilty—and not quite sure why—Cassie had left the building, relieved to find the promised car waiting for her at the Brompton Road entrance to the store. But the only person in the vast vehicle was the chauffeur and she found herself wishing that Giancarlo had come to collect her personally. Maybe he wasn't the kind of man who sat waiting patiently for a woman—but it didn't exactly do her ego much good.

And now she felt a bit like a door-to-door salesperson as she made her way up the flight of white stairs leading to the enormous front door, the candles in one hand, her fingers clutching tightly at her handbag with the other. What on earth was she going to talk to him about? But before she'd had the chance to ring the bell, the door opened and there was Giancarlo himself—a gleam flickering in the depths of his ebony eyes.

His black hair was gleaming and tousled—as if he'd run his fingers through it when he'd been fresh out of the shower—and he wore a fine white silk shirt which was unbuttoned at the neck. Dark trousers hugged his narrow hips and emphasised the muscular legs and he seemed much taller than she remembered. Despite the simplicity of his clothes, he looked rich and powerful and intimidatingly masculine and Cassie felt the sudden spiralling of nerves.

'So here you are,' he said softly.

'Here I am.' Glad to have something to distract her, she thrust the package into his hand. 'Look, I've brought your candles.'

His lips curved into a smile as he took them from her. Candles were the very last thing on his mind. '*Grazie*. Now come inside and let me look at *you*.' Giancarlo's throat thickened as she stepped past him into the hallway on those killer heels, with a sway of her silken hair.

He let his gaze drift over her. Even when she'd been working behind the counter in her starchy uniform with her hair scraped back there had been some quality about her which had intrigued him. But in the short dress and high heels with that pale cascade of blonde hair running down her back, she looked utterly irresistible. Fresh, and young and firm. Suddenly, he wished he knew her well enough to skip dinner and take her straight to bed. Or at least to start kissing her. 'You look amazing,' he said softly as he put the package down on a table.

'Do I?'

'You know you do.'

But Cassie shrugged a little awkwardly. Like most women, she had little real confidence in the way she looked—even though she'd tried her best to fit in since arriving in London and discovering that her Cornish clothes weren't really suitable for a city lifestyle. Sometimes it felt as if she'd taken on a different persona to match the new outfits she'd acquired—a glossy patina which concealed the real her. She'd certainly never have worn heels this high or a dress this short back home. But then, she'd never have been standing looking into the face of a man like this back home, would she?

Suddenly shy and wanting to divert herself from the gleam of appraisal in his black eyes, she glanced around the entrance hall, which was as big as a room itself with its high ceilings and pale grey walls hung with a series of muted charcoal drawings of a beautiful Japanese woman. Stained glass from the window light of the front door splashed reds and blues on the tiled black and white floor, and on a gleaming rosewood table stood a glass bowl of white roses and freesia which perfumed the air with their delicate scent. The airy dimensions and sense of space were awesome—it was like somewhere you might see in one of those glossy interior magazines you found at the dentist's—and Cassie couldn't imagine just one person living in a place this big.

She looked at Giancarlo expectantly, waiting for him to fetch his jacket. 'Where are we going for dinner?' she asked.

'Well, actually, we're not going anywhere.' His voice was soft. 'We're eating right here.'

'Here?' Her heart began to thud and she wasn't sure why. She had imagined a rooftop and a twinkling city view. Someone playing a white piano—and cocktail waitresses with flowers in their hair. The soft murmur of conversation and watching all the rich people out at play.

'You have some sort of objection to that, *mia bella*?' His eyes gleamed. 'You don't think the standard of food will be what you're used to?'

Her cheeks grew pink at the mockery in his voice. 'Well, I...'

'Well, what, Cassandra?' he questioned teasingly.

Nobody—*nobody*—ever called her Cassandra. And nobody had ever told her that an Italian voice could make a single word sound like a soft seduction. Surely it wasn't decent behaviour for her to have dinner alone in a man's house on their first date—and yet if she came out and told him so, then wouldn't it make her sound awfully naïve? As if she'd just come up from the country and were some sort of *hick*. Maybe this was normal behaviour for London. And just because they were eating in didn't mean he was going to leap on her, did it? Cassie cleared her throat. 'I just thought—well, there are lots of lovely restaurants locally.'

'So there are—but most of them are full of tourists and office parties at this time of the year.' He held out his hand towards her. 'Come with me and let me see if I can change your mind.'

She let him take her hand and allowed him to lead her along an endless corridor hung with yet more pictures, past the faint sound of a radio and the clanking sound of something being whisked. The corridor led into an enormous, wooden-floored room dotted with several dramatic sculptures and large French windows which opened onto a beautiful conservatory, where a table had been set for dinner.

Stars gleamed through the clear ceiling, a bottle of champagne sat waiting in an ice-bucket and pots of jasmine scented the air. Aware that he was still holding her hand and that it now seemed a little too intimate, Cassie shook hers free and walked over to the glass doors, which overlooked an enormous garden.

Though the night was cold and dark, strategic lights had been placed around the huge grounds, illuminating bare trees and elegant shrubs so that the whole scene resembled a winter stage-set. It was the prettiest and most unexpected thing she had ever seen—as if the countryside had been transplanted into the centre of the busy city and given a theatrical twist.

'Oh, my,' she breathed. 'All that garden—and right in the middle of London. Lucky you.'

Luck? Giancarlo walked over to stand beside her, looking at the tight high curve of her young bottom as he did so and the way the pale blonde hair fell almost to her waist. How people always looked at his life and thought he'd had it easy. He thought that luck didn't feature as strongly as the capricious hand of fate and a corresponding determination to make something of himself. The senseless shock of a double betrayal. And the long, grim struggle to work his way up from the bottom. To prove to his brother and himself that he didn't need an inheritance to elevate himself to the level of a wealthy man.

And he had done it. Exceeded even his own exacting standards and lofty expectations. Been single-minded enough to focus on his goal and to achieve the success he had set out to achieve. Which was why he could bring this beautiful young woman into his home—for a meal which would rival most award-winning restaurants in the capital.

'So have you changed your mind about going out? Can you think of anywhere prettier to eat?' he questioned, glancing at the waterfall of blonde hair which was rippling down her narrow back.

'I guess I can't. Not really. But who's doing the cooking?'

'Well, not me, that's for sure!' Walking back over to the table, he pulled the bottle of champagne from the bucket and removed the thick foil with his thumb. 'Drink?'

'Lovely,' she said lightly, taking the flute of pale fizz from him and giving a little squeak as she sipped it.

'Bubbles up your nose?' he murmured.

'Every time,' she agreed sanguinely, as if she drank champagne every day of her life. 'So who *does* do your cooking?'

'I have staff.' His tone was casual. 'A cook. A housekeeper. A gardener.'

'Gosh. How very indulgent.'

He flicked her a glance. Wealth did strange things. It opened up the world like an oyster—and closed off other parts of it for ever. It isolated and enclosed you in a rarefied and gilded existence. It meant that people sometimes looked at you with envy—or avarice. But that was the price you paid. And what would this little shop-girl know of his life unless he told her? 'More a necessity than an indulgence. I travel a lot for work and my hours are long. So I don't have time for all the maintenance stuff.'

'And even if you did—maybe you still wouldn't do it? I can't really imagine you peeling potatoes or hammering a nail in a wall.'

'The former is what I'd expect a woman to do,' he said, with a faint glimmer of a smile. 'The hammering part of the equation wouldn't be a problem.'

Cassie nearly choked on the mouthful of champagne she was drinking. 'You're not serious?'

'About the nail? Sure I am. I'm pretty good with a hammer.'

She blushed—because the soft mockery in his voice made it sound as though he was referring to something other than DIY skills. 'I meant your remark about peeling potatoes being women's work.'

'Are you going to subject me to a lecture about sexual stereotypes, *bella*?' he mocked. 'Because let me save you the time. I know it off by heart.'

Cassie stared at him, her heart beating very fast. 'Some people might describe that as arrogance, Giancarlo.'

'Guilty as charged,' he said silkily.

Cassie stared at him and their eyes clashed—fighting a sudden silent battle which had nothing to do with potatoes or sexual stereotypes. A battle which was completely alien to her—and yet one for which she was suddenly discovering an instinctive knowledge.

Yet another type of intuition was telling her that she was in danger—a subtle and insidious kind. The kind of danger which was making her want to behave with an abandon she wasn't even aware she possessed. She knew exactly what she *should* do. Turn around and walk right out of there. Away from the temptation of an arrogant and heartbreakingly handsome man with his servants and his wealth and his crushing contempt for women.

But something stopped her. The same thing which had first made her heart leap with some kind of primitive recognition the first time she'd set eyes on him. An attraction which wasn't based on intellect or reason or understanding—but on something much more fundamental.

Desire.

Shakily, she put her glass down on the table. 'I don't think I'd better have any more to drink on any empty stomach,' she said.

Giancarlo had seen the darkening of her eyes, felt the unmistakable crackle of tension between them and known that there had been a moment when she had longed for him to take her in his arms and kiss her. The moment was lost—but almost certainly there would be another. 'Then let's eat. Are you hungry?'

'Starving,' she said, without much enthusiasm.

Cassie watched as he walked back over to the French windows and, reaching inside, rang some sort of bell. He's ringing a bell to summon his servants! she thought. Once again, she could feel a slightly hysterical sense of being divorced from reality—as a dark-haired woman he introduced as Gina carried out a dish and laid it in the centre of the table, soon followed by a bowl of potatoes and platter of green beans.

'Just something simple,' he said softly as he pulled out a chair for Cassie. 'Which will leave you plenty of room for dessert.'

Cassie didn't know whether she was imagining

sensual imagery at every corner and whether he was intending for that to happen. All she did know was that the woman called Gina was making her feel uncomfortable. Tall and slim, with a pair of trendy black-rimmed spectacles perched on her nose, she was aged about forty and spoke briefly to Giancarlo in Italian.

So was it the language exclusion which made Cassie feel so out of place—or the fear that Gina might be judging her? Maybe it was her own guilty conscience making her feel awkward as she wondered just how many women had sat where she was sitting, dining with a wealthy Italian they'd only just met. Did any of them stay the night, she wondered—and did Gina serve coffee and breakfast in the morning as if nothing had happened?

'Cassie?' Giancarlo's voice broke into the swirl of her thoughts.

'Sorry?' Biting her lip, she looked up at him to find his ebony gaze washing over her. What on earth was she *doing*—thinking about women staying the night here?

'You were miles away.'

'Was I?' She helped herself to a portion of chicken from the dish he was holding towards her. 'Sorry, I was just thinking...'

'What were you thinking?'

Hastily, Cassie reassembled her thoughts, glad that the candlelight hid her sudden rise in colour. 'That I've never met anyone who has staff before. Gina's Italian, isn't she?'

'Yes, she is.'

'And what about the others that you mentioned—the cook and the gardener—are they all Italian?'

'Do you want me to go through the CVs of my entire staff?' he questioned softly, taking the bowl from her and placing it in the middle of the table. 'Yes, they are all Italian. They've been with me a long time and know my tastes. Now relax, *bella*—and eat your dinner. I'm much more interested to hear about you and how you came to be working at the store.'

'Really?'

'Yes, really.'

'Well, I live in Cornwall—I may have mentioned that.'

'And what is it like, living in Cornwall?' he murmured.

She shot him a shy look. 'Oh, it's *gorgeous*—with the most beautiful beaches and the biggest waves you've ever seen. It's a surfers' paradise and does the best cream teas in the world—have you never been there?'

'No, I haven't.' His lips curved, because her enthusiasm was really very sweet. 'Tell me more.'

'I live close to the sea—in Trevone,' she said.

'On your own?'

'No, with my mother. She runs a B&B—that's bed and breakfast—though there are hardly any guests during the winter. My father...' She swallowed. 'Well, my father died a couple of years ago.'

'I'm sorry.'

'Thank you.' Cassie put her fork down. People always said that. *I'm sorry.* As if somehow they were responsible for the death of a stranger. She guessed it was just what people said when they didn't really know what to say—though she couldn't imagine that Giancarlo Vellutini was often stuck for words. She shot him a quick glance as he ate a mouthful of chicken and pushed a bit more food around on her own plate. 'I suppose you're shocked that a woman my age is still living at home?'

He shook his head and shrugged. It meant that there would be no liaisons in her home town—but so what? He wasn't planning long-term.

'I am from Italy,' he said softly. 'Where such a scenario is common. Living with your parents has many advantages—for both parties—although, naturally, it can curtail individual freedom.'

She couldn't have put it better herself. 'Exactly!'

'Is that why you came to London, Cassandra? Because you wanted to be free?'

'Yes, well—sort of,' she said slowly—because only now had her mother come out of her frozen grief, and allowed Cassie to think that it was okay to leave her on her own. But it was more than that. Hadn't her father's death made her rethink everything? Hadn't it brought home how frighteningly fragile life was and made her examine her own and find it wanting? Making her realise that it was whizzing by and she had done very little with it. 'I wanted a break. Felt I was in a bit of a rut. You know.'

She paused to allow him to agree, but he didn't—and when she thought about it, a jet-setting man like him was unlikely to get bored with the daily grind, was he?

'You see, I've only ever lived in one place and felt it was time for a change,' she continued. 'I work in a shop in Padstow—a really pretty little gift shop which sells trinkets and craft kits and fancy food. Cornish clotted-cream biscuits and crystals—that sort of thing. I'd like to get promoted to manageress—and the owner said that it might be a good idea if I got a bit of experience in London first. She knows one of the buyers at Hudson's—and she arranged for me to get a temporary job there during the Christmas rush. And so, here I am.'

'Here you are,' he agreed, sitting back in his chair and looking at her. 'With your eyes the colour of those little bunches of violets you sometimes see on city market stalls—all dewy fresh amid the dust and grime.'

She blushed and glanced down at her plate, feeling the sudden skitter of her heart. 'I wish you wouldn't say things like that.'

'But surely men say that kind of thing to you all the time, especially if you blush so enchantingly in response.'

'Not really.'

'No? Oh, come on, Cassandra—I can't believe there isn't a long line of men beating a path to your door.'

Cassie supposed it would sound shaming to admit that few men of her acquaintance had offered little more in the way of flattery than a terse 'not bad' when she'd dressed up for a date. But then most of the men she met were those she'd grown up with who felt more like brothers—or married men who came into the shop accompanied by their wife and two toddlers. Tentatively, she raised her eyes to meet the mocking question in his. 'I don't think Englishmen are quite as…well, as…*verbal* as Italians.'

He smiled. 'Ah, so now we're talking *national* stereotypes, are we? You prefer the Italian male with his innate ability to charm women?'

'That sounds more like boasting than charming to me!'

His eyes glittered. 'And that sounds as if you're laying down a challenge, my beauty.'

Cassie swallowed as he made that silky declaration—aware that the strangest sensations were washing over her and there didn't seem to be a thing she could do to stop them. She wanted him to kiss her—and they hadn't even finished their main courses. And wasn't there also *another* characteristic attributed to Italian men—that they didn't respect women who gave into them too easily?

'I think…I think that champagne is going to my head. May I have a glass of water, please?' she questioned weakly, because why on earth was she leaping ahead of herself like this and thinking about 'giving in' to him? As if it would take any persuasion at all! Again, she could feel the heated prickling of her skin—and if Giancarlo Vellutini had the slightest inkling what was going on inside her head he would think her insane!

'Of course.' Reading the darkening of desire in her eyes, Giancarlo poured her a glass, approving of the fact that she wasn't much of a drinker. He didn't want alcohol blurring her reactions or influencing her judgement tonight—or any sense of false outrage in the morning. He wanted her and she wanted him—the only question was whether she was honest enough to admit it. 'You haven't eaten very much.'

'No. I'm not really hungry. What a terrible dinner guest I am.'

'I'm certainly not complaining,' he murmured. 'Do I take it you're not in the market for dessert?'

Cassie shook her head. Normally, she loved puddings—the sweeter and creamier, the better—but right now she felt as if anything else to eat might choke her. 'Not really. Well, not just yet. I hope it won't offend Gina.'

He shook his head. 'I don't employ Gina to get offended. Maybe a walk might give you an appetite?'

'A walk? Where would we walk?'

He pointed to the shadows falling over the lawn,

which was now growing white with frost. 'If you look outside there's a great big garden at our feet.' His eyes glanced down at the vertiginous heels which made her fragile ankles look almost impossibly slender. 'Though speaking of feet—I don't think those shoes were made for walking.'

She followed the direction of his gaze. 'No. I think you could be right.'

'Pity. You should have worn trainers.'

'Trainers would have looked terrible with this dress.'

He laughed. 'True. Never mind, *bella*—perhaps I will take you for a walk another time.'

But Cassie felt as if a wonderful opportunity was slipping away from her. Suddenly, she became aware that this evening would never happen again—hadn't the way he'd said 'perhaps' driven that simple fact home? That it didn't matter where she went in life or what she did—there would never be another frosty December evening in Kensington with this particular man.

He was the most captivating person she'd ever met and he had liked *her* enough to ask her to dinner. And nothing was certain. After tonight, she might never see him again. And if that were to be the case, then wouldn't she have wasted the most wonderful opportunity to see how the other half lived? Too choked up with nerves to be able to enjoy herself properly—and too constrained by her impulsive shoe purchase to be able to appreciate the beautiful gardens of his home.

'Oh, I'm not going to be put off by a stupid pair of high heels!' she declared. 'Haven't you got an old pair of wellington boots that I could borrow?'

Impulsively, she bent and untied the ankle strap,

slipping off one of the shoes in a move which left her curiously lopsided. Smiling up at him, she reached for the other strap but something stopped her. Or rather—someone.

For Giancarlo had bent before her—almost, she thought dazedly, like a man about to propose marriage. And he was undoing the other strap—only he was taking much longer than she had done. His thumb was circling at her insole as he slid the shoe off in a movement which felt unbelievably erotic…like a slow shoe-striptease. And now his hand was sliding up her ankle, and her calf.

'Bare legs,' he murmured approvingly. 'That's what I like about English and American girls—they have bare legs in winter. Even better than stockings.'

His fingertips had now reached the back of her knee—just one light touch and she had begun to tremble uncontrollably. 'Giancarlo—'

'What?' If it weren't the first time then he would have continued with his erotic journey. Brought her to orgasm with his fingers and then perhaps have followed it with the slow lick of his tongue—before carrying her off to his bedroom for a long night of pleasure. But it was the first time, and so he straightened up—finding that she looked so much smaller without her heels. And so delicate.

With the stars beginning to sprinkle the dark sky above them and the rise of the moon making a pale halo of her hair, she looked as if some flower fairy had tumbled down and taken up residence within the airy confines of his conservatory. Lightly, he placed his hands at her waist as if to anchor her down—thinking that if he let her go she might simply drift away.

'Wh-what about the boots?' she questioned.

'What about them?' he repeated unevenly as he let his fingers drift up towards the luscious swell of her breasts.

'Aren't we…supposed to be going outside for a walk before pudding?'

'I've changed my mind.'

Aware that things were proceeding with a rapidity she hadn't anticipated, Cassie felt a sudden flurry of nerves. 'You…you've let me chatter about myself all evening and yet you haven't told me anything about yourself.'

'Like what?' he murmured.

'Oh, I don't know.' Cassie swallowed as he pulled her closer—so that she could feel the heat of his body and the warmth of his breath. 'Your…your life. Your work. Your dreams.'

Her words shattered his fantasy. Giancarlo's mouth hardened with a grim kind of reality check—and not just because talking was the last thing on his mind right now. Start telling a woman about your dreams and she started seeing happy-ever-after. And what if he told her that he had no dreams left? Wouldn't that only make her determined to prove him wrong in that way that women had—wanting to show that they and only they could change you? And they couldn't—even if you wanted them to. 'There's only one thing you need to know about me, Cassandra,' he said softly.

She turned her face upwards, part of her knowing what he was about to say. And although there were a million questions bubbling beneath the surface, it was as if she were programmed to ask the only one which mattered. 'What's that?' she whispered hesitantly.

'This.' And his lips came down to meet hers in a crushing kiss.

CHAPTER THREE

GIANCARLO's bedroom was vast. Big and intimidating as an ocean—so that for a moment Cassie felt like a tiny little raft bobbing around in unknown territory, unsure which direction to take. Down on his terrace where he had been kissing her and kissing her until their breath had mingled and they had been wrapped tightly in each other's arms, she had felt no qualms. As he had tangled his fingers in the spill of her hair beneath the rising moon she had felt as though she had found her place in the world. A magical place which was governed by feeling and by the irresistible lure of the senses.

But then the kissing had become more frantic. She had felt the urgent clamour of her body and dimly recognised the growing need in his. And that had been the moment when he had stopped kissing her, his lips moving instead to her ear.

'If we don't stop this right now, *mia bella*, then I will take you right here—and I think we should be more comfortable for our first time together, don't you?'

The sexual declaration had been stark, and it should have been scary—especially for someone of Cassie's experience. But her heart had been pounding so wildly and her body so tense and trembling with desire for him that she hadn't been able to do anything other than nod and let him take her by the hand as he had done at the very start of the evening. Only this time he led her through the huge and echoing house—up the majestic sweep of a mighty staircase to his bedroom.

And now that she was here, Cassie was suddenly filled with nerves at the thought of what was about to happen. That maybe she would disappoint him. Or that he would think she had capitulated much too easily. And she had, hadn't she?

'Cassandra, *bella*.' Sensing her restraint, he pulled her back into his arms and tilted her face upwards, stroking away a bright strand of hair which had fallen over her cheek as he looked down at her. 'You have changed your mind? You don't want me?'

What could she say? Cross her fingers and tell a lie? Could she really bear to do that—shrug her shoulders with embarrassment and say she'd got a little carried away and had changed her mind?

Because he would let her. He might not have told her anything about his life or his work or his dreams, but something told Cassie that he was not only honourable enough to let her go—but proud enough never to ask her back again. And she would spend the rest of her life asking herself the most painful question of all. *What if?*

'Yes, I want you,' she whispered.

Giancarlo smiled as he felt the rush of uncomplicated pleasure. 'Then isn't it convenient that I happen to want you, too?' he questioned unsteadily. 'Do you want to know how much?'

'Giancarlo…' Her eyes closed as his mouth drifted down to the hollow above her shoulder blade.

'This much.'

She moaned as his hand cupped her breast over the soft material of her dress and then found the side-zip of her dress and slid it down—his lips grazing over hers in erotic dance all the while. And she moaned again as he peeled the garment over her head and she felt the rush of air to her partially bare skin. Because suddenly she was standing there in her underwear—her nipples peaking and her thighs tingling. Her body was on fire and she was clinging to him as his lips and his hands trailed pure delight over her skin. Should she warn him? she wondered dazedly.

She swallowed as his palms cupped her bottom and he pulled her closer. 'Giancarlo—'

'I want to study you,' he murmured. 'I want to examine every inch of you—to know you so well that if I were to take an exam about your body then I would get full marks. But the trouble is that my desire for you is so great that I think we might have to postpone that pleasure until later,' he declared, his voice thick with desire as he guided her trembling fingers to his shirt buttons. Because it had been a long time, he realised. A long time since he had wanted a woman as much as this. 'Undo my shirt.'

Her hands were trembling so much that it felt like an almost impossible task—until her first encounter with the silky texture of his flesh. And suddenly her doubts melted away and she became greedy. Like a prospector who had suddenly found an abundance of gold, Cassie found herself wanting to run her fingers all over his hair-roughened torso. She felt him twist slightly as she ran her fingertips over his flesh, heard him give a little laugh as she touched each of his diamond-hard nipples.

'You are making me forget the reason I brought you up here,' he growled. 'Which was to take you to bed.' And, picking her up, he carried her across the room to the biggest bed Cassie had ever seen.

He laid her down upon it, his dark eyes not leaving hers as he pulled off his clothes—until he was wearing nothing but a pair of dark silk boxer shorts. Cassie could see the flagrant ridge at the front of them and suddenly she began to shiver. This was really happening—and she was letting it happen. *Should* she tell him? Wasn't it wrong *not* to tell him?

'You tremble. You are cold?' he murmured. This was asked as he joined her, dragging a huge coverlet over them and pulling her close against his warm body.

'N-no, I'm not cold.'

'Me, neither. In fact, I think we are both wearing too much, don't you? Shall we do something about that?' Unclipping her bra, he tossed it aside and then began to slide her panties down over her thighs, his fingertips whispering enticing little paths along the way, which made her gasp. And then he removed his boxers—edged them off with his feet and gave a shuddering sigh as he felt her nakedness next to his. How long had it been since he had lain with a woman? Long enough for his breath to catch strangely in his throat with an odd sense of *discovery* as he stroked her delicate skin.

He looked down at her—at the way her long, blonde hair lay spread out over his pillow like a silken cloud. At the curved, feminine body—with its luscious breasts and rounded hips. She was like a goddess, he thought. Yet a goddess who was giving herself to him with sweet abandon. 'You are beautiful, Cassandra,' he murmured. 'And I am a lucky man.'

'Kiss me,' she whispered.

Softly, his mouth came down and covered hers. He could feel her body melting into his, her fingers tangling in his hair and the increasingly restless movement of her hips as the kiss deepened. At last he lifted his head and traced the outline of her lips with the tip of his finger. 'Don't go away.'

Her eyes opened wide in alarm as he pulled away from her. 'Where…where are you going?'

'Not far.'

He had leaned across the bed to pull something from the drawer of a gleaming antique table—and it was only when he had ripped the packet open and begun to slide on a condom that Cassie realised what he was doing.

Tell him.

Tell him.

But now he was moving over her and kissing her again and it all seemed so perfect—and wouldn't it break the mood if she came right out and told him? With a groan and a whispering of her name, he parted her legs and she could feel the rocky tip of him pushing against her molten heat.

'Giancarlo—'

'*Sì?*' he breathed raggedly.

'It's…it's my first time,' she gasped, just as he thrust inside her.

Giancarlo shuddered—but he was in too deep to stop, even as he felt her tense and her nails dig into his shoulders. And even if he'd wanted to, he couldn't have stopped. Not if the world had been about to end. Or maybe that was what was happening. Because now she was clutching him tightly, bringing him into her deeper still—her breath hot on his neck as she bit out his name.

Her molten tightness sent heated flares of desire rippling through him—devouring him with their intensity as he moved inside her. Never before had he wanted to come quite so much—but he made himself hold back. Using every skill he'd learnt since he lost his own virginity at sixteen, he drove Cassandra closer and closer towards her own sweet oblivion. Didn't they say it was difficult for a virgin to achieve orgasm the first time? Well, he would make sure that he proved the statistics wrong, he thought grimly—watching her eyes close as she began to abandon herself to the siren call of fulfilment.

Over and over again, he drew back from the brink—until finally he heard her little cry of disbelief and felt her arch beneath him. Never before could he remember feeling such an intense sense of satisfaction as when she gasped and began to spasm around him—and only when at last she had begun to still beneath him did he allow himself his own release. A release which went on and on—his pleasure only heightened by the anger and disbelief which began to ripple through him as he thought of what he had done.

Afterwards, he rolled off her and turned over onto his side, propping himself up on his elbow and taking a moment or two before he could control his breathing enough to speak. And to block out the appeal of her sated beauty—her tousled hair and flushed cheeks and the parted invitation of her breathless lips. 'That was some surprise you sprang on me, *cara*.'

Cassie's fingers fluttered to her breastbone as she registered the dark note of disapproval in his voice. 'You mean—about me being a virgin?'

'No, I mean about you being a natural blonde,' he drawled sarcastically.

Her warm glow and slightly dreamy sensation rapidly began to evaporate and she bit her lip. 'I should have told you.'

Hardening his heart to the anxiety in her violet eyes, he nodded his head in violent agreement. 'Well, actually you *did* tell me—only you left it too late for me to do anything about it,' he growled. Too late for him to do anything but thrust deep inside her with a sense of powerlessness which had overwhelmed him. Because he didn't do powerlessness. Not any more.

She looked up into the hard glitter of his black eyes. 'Would you...would you have stopped then?'

For a moment he didn't answer. He wanted to say that yes, he would have stopped—but would he? Could he? If she had mentioned it on the terrace before she had come so eagerly with him to bed—he could have resisted her then, that was for sure. But she hadn't. She had waited until they were at a point of no return before she had blurted out her unbelievable statement.

'What the hell are you doing letting a man take your virginity from you on a first date?' he demanded.

He was acting as if she had done something *wrong*— shameful even. 'Somebody has to take it,' she said flatly.

'But not like *that*. Not with a man you barely know.' A man who has no intention of forming any kind of deep or lasting relationship with you. Exasperatedly, he shook his head. 'How old are you?'

'Twenty-one.'

So young, he thought bitterly—and yet surely old enough to have had some sexual experience before.

'And there's been no one else?' He gave a hollow kind of laugh. 'Stupid question. I've just proved the answer to that one.' He could ask her *why him*, but you wouldn't be a genius to be able to work *that* one out and he was a fool not to have seen it before.

She was gorgeous, yes—but her looks had not yet had the power to lift her from her rather mundane circumstances and elevate her to the kind of lifestyle which such beauty merited. Was that breathless and rather sweet attitude carefully cultivated? Because maybe she had been clever enough to realise that her distinctive looks were a gift from the gods which should not be squandered. That they could be used as a bargaining tool in the oldest barter-game in the world—beauty in exchange for riches.

Was that the real reason why she'd found herself a job in a chi-chi department store in one of the wealthiest areas of London? Hoping that some rich and ardent suitor would come walking in and whisk her away from it all? She must have been holding out for the highest bidder—the richest suitor to enter her radar—because what other reason would a woman have for giving away her precious virginity with such ease?

Giancarlo's mouth hardened. And he had walked right into it. For someone who had acquired a sixth sense where gold-diggers were concerned—whose whole life had been shaped by one—he had been like putty in her hands. Bewitched by a pair of huge violet eyes and a pair of rose-petal lips and an unusual combination of shyness and sass.

Reeling from the sudden contempt in his eyes, Cassie sat up in bed, wanting to get away—terrified that she was going to do something stupid. Like cry. Or wonder aloud how she could have been such a gullible idiot to allow herself to get into such a situation with a man it was now clear had nothing but disdain for her. 'No, there's been no one else! And I'm sorry I've been such a disappointment to you, but don't worry, Giancarlo—I won't bother you ever again.'

Flinging the rumpled coverlet off her, she wriggled towards the end of the bed, but Giancarlo reached out and captured her with a hand to her naked hip.

'Where do you think you're going?'

'Home! Let me go! I didn't think that it was such a *terrible* sin to make love with a man. Why didn't you interrogate me beforehand to check that I fulfilled all your obviously strict criteria? No virgins need apply! Now will you please let go of me?'

'No.' His voice was firm and his hold on her unwavering. 'You're not going anywhere.'

'Are you going to keep me here against my will?'

He gave a hollow laugh. 'I think you may be taking the innocent virgin theme a little too far,' he said drily as he pulled her warm body back into his arms. 'I'm not intending to keep you prisoner here against your will. Come back here, Cassandra—and don't fight me just because you feel you ought to, when we both know you don't want to.'

The awful thing was that he was right—she *didn't* want to fight him. She wanted to nestle in his arms and she wanted him to start kissing her all over again. Or at least—that was what her body wanted. But her mind was telling her something entirely different. It was telling her to be proud and strong and to get away while she could because this dark and dangerous man could lead her into all kinds of trouble. 'Leave me alone!' she whispered.

'No.' His kissed her—felt her brief resistance as she tried to fight it, but her lips parted beneath his within seconds. A woman's kiss tasted different once you'd made love to her, he reflected—it was scented with arousal and warm with intimacy. He felt the renewed flicker of desire as his tongue flicked against hers in sensual duel before drawing his head away to look down into her dazed face. 'Just tell me one thing. A woman who looks like you…still a virgin. How come? There must have been a million men who wanted you before I came along.'

She felt that she shouldn't have to *explain* herself—not to him—not to anyone. But pride made her want to, if only to prove that she wasn't some kind of tramp, but a woman who had made a judgement and wouldn't have regretted a moment of it if only he hadn't been reacting like this.

'Not a million men, no,' she said slowly, because the fierce light from his black eyes was demanding some kind of answer to his question. 'Some—of course. But a lot of them were men I'd grown up with—and they were more like brothers, really.'

'And that's it?' he questioned coolly. 'The sum total of your experience?'

'Not quite all—I've had a few…' She hesitated, until she realised that the fixed ebony spotlight of his eyes wasn't moving. 'Well, married men hitting on me.'

His eyes narrowed. Yes, he could imagine that. She, who looked like sin and temptation, would make the perfect mistress for a man locked into a dead relationship who was looking for a little bit of sweet diversion on the side. Yet who would have thought that beneath that mouth-watering exterior beat the heart of a virgin?

Former virgin, he reminded himself grimly. 'But you weren't interested?'

Cassie's mouth tightened with derision. 'Funnily enough—no. I've never considered it acceptable behaviour to go off with another woman's husband.'

'Yet for all you know—I could have a wife tucked away somewhere,' he challenged softly, and held her gaze.

It only took a couple of seconds before Cassie shook her head. 'No.'

'No? So sure, Cassandra?'

'Sure enough. You don't strike me as the kind of dishonourable man who would do that kind of thing.'

Giancarlo flinched. How ridiculously trusting she was— and how misplaced that trust! Why did she think he was particularly honourable after what had just happened? When he had brought her here with nothing but seduction in mind. And something in the way she spoke nagged at his conscience—the proud look on her face making him think that this was no gold-digger who had taken a job in a fancy store to trawl for a rich lover.

But why else would she give her virginity to a man who was little more than a stranger to her?

Stroking the flat of his hand down over the silken spill of her hair, he leaned closer and suddenly the scent of desire mixed with her own particular perfume sent lust arrowing through him. 'Are you going to let me kiss you again?'

She shook her head. 'No. You've made it clear that you think the whole evening has been a mistake—and the best thing for all concerned is for me to get dressed and get out of here.'

'Are you sure about that?'

'Y-yes.'

His hand moved down to comfortably cup a breast between his fingers. 'Quite sure?'

Confronted by his rugged face in close-up, his body warm against hers, Cassie felt her determination begin to slip away. Enthralled by the sudden siren call of her new-awakened body, she felt helpless to do anything other than melt against him while he continued to play with her nipple. 'I shouldn't,' she whispered.

'Sì. You should. For it is too late now for recriminations. We should make the most of what we have done by exploring a few more possibilities...don't you think?'

'Yes,' she breathed as his mouth touched hers again and her hand fluttered to one firm, silky-hard buttock.

'Oh, Cassandra,' he groaned. 'Sì, ah—sì!'

This time it was different. This time he showed her that love-making wasn't always frantic and urgent—but could be long and slow and deep. And afterwards he brought her very close against him while her trembling body grew still.

Cradling her head on his chest, Cassie could hear the powerful beat of his heart and hear the slowing of his breath—and suddenly she wanted reassurance. For him to tell her that what they'd done wasn't wrong.

'Giancarlo?' she murmured.

'Shh. Don't spoil it by talking,' he instructed softly. 'Just sleep.'

She thought there were more diplomatic ways to respond to a woman but she was too tired to object. Her body was weary—worn out by the new sensations it had experienced, and she was worn out by emotion, too. So she heeded his words and let her eyelids flutter down and sleep claim her.

* * *

When Cassie awoke, it took a few moments for her to realise where she was. A rumpled bed in a huge room with light spilling in from a pair of enormous windows. A little way off she could hear the sound of a shower and she must have drifted off to sleep again because when next she opened her eyes it was to see Giancarlo standing on the opposite side of the room, fully dressed. He was wearing a dark suit and another pristine white silk shirt—and was in the process of knotting a grey-and rose-coloured tie as their eyes met.

Suddenly Cassie felt shy. More than that—she felt disorientated. And alone. Had he woken, eager to vacate the bed and the woman who had given herself to him so easily?

Their eyes met for a long moment and he crossed the room to plant a quick kiss on her lips. 'Good morning,' he said softly.

'Good morning.' But the kiss had felt more perfunctory than passionate, Cassie thought. She looked up at his crisp, cool morning image and the naked man who had taken her to heaven and back during the night now seemed to have left the building. *What the hell did she do next?*

'Would you like a shower?' he asked, as if he'd tuned into her thoughts, and then his voice softened as he ran his fingers through her tousled hair. 'Don't look so disappointed, *cara*. This isn't the kind of awakening I'd have chosen, but you were sleeping so peacefully that I couldn't bear to wake you—and, unfortunately, I have an early meeting.'

Yet even as he said it Giancarlo knew that wasn't the whole truth. For hadn't he woken with regrets on his mind—even while his body had been hardening with renewed desire for her? He had taken her virginity, and, even though he had made her sexual initiation as satisfactory as he knew how, the situation was fraught with danger. She might form an attachment to him which he would be unable to reciprocate—and any brief affair they might have would be complicated by his own feelings of responsibility, and guilt. So wouldn't it be better to make a clean break? To let her go now before she got in any deeper—and he hurt her, as he would inevitably hurt her. He tucked a strand of hair behind her ear.

'Or you could always have a bath, if you preferred?' he murmured.

Somehow Cassie managed a smile—because you wouldn't need to be a woman of the world to realise that when a man was besotted with you, he didn't feel the need to talk about the plumbing arrangements. She sensed what was coming. A polite but very definite farewell. But she wasn't going to cling—or to come over as needy. She had walked into this scenario with little thought about dignity—but it wasn't too late to resurrect some now.

'Don't worry about a thing—I'm due in at nine. I'll have a shower and then I'll go straight to work.'

'Good. Well, Gina will serve you breakfast—just tell her what it is you'd like.'

Cassie couldn't think of anything worse than the cool-looking Italian woman serving her breakfast—and with her still wearing the same clothes that she'd worn the night before. 'Thanks,' she said politely.

'And my driver will take you wherever you want to go.'

Cassie shook her head. This was awful—just *awful*—this self-conscious chit-chat as if what had happened during the night hadn't happened at all. As if she hadn't been writhing beneath him while his mouth had explored hers with a sweet passion. 'No, honestly—I'm going to work and it's not far. And the walk will do me good,' she finished.

Their eyes met during a silence which grew in awkwardness by the moment—and yet what on earth could she say to break it? wondered Cassie desperately. Especially when the only words on her lips were ones of bittersweet regret that she should have allowed herself to get so carried away and to have lost her virginity to a man who clearly regretted taking it.

'I'll ring you,' he said slowly.

Cassie nodded. But she knew with a horrible aching certainty that he never would. He'd got what he'd wanted and now it was perfectly plain that he couldn't wait to get away. She fixed what she hoped was a nonchalant smile on her lips, because she was all out of bright and breezy responses. And she didn't dare move. He might have encouraged her to act with uninhibited pleasure in his arms countless times throughout the night—but *no way* was she going to walk naked across the room in front of him.

Maybe he sensed her discomfiture, because he left without another word. And once she heard the sound of the front door slamming shut, Cassie quickly got out of bed and made use of the en-suite bathroom, her mind too full to register the unfamiliar luxury which awaited her there.

At least she felt marginally better once she'd showered—even though it was no fun putting on the same clothes and underwear—but at least she wore a uniform at work and she could nip out in her lunch-hour and buy another pair of pants.

The morning was winter at its most beautiful—the sky icy-blue and the frost in the park coating every blade of grass with a layer of ice-white. She tried to count her blessings. To tell herself that it was a once-in-a-lifetime experience that she would never forget and that she would soon get over it. Well, there was nothing much to get over, was there?

Was it her imagination, or did the usually friendly doorman in front of the glossy gold and claret façade which was Hudson's look at her rather oddly—or was she getting paranoid? Just because she had probably made the biggest mistake of her life—didn't mean that she had to start imagining things.

Taking the lift down to the basement, she went towards the changing rooms but before she could push the door open two figures stepped forward to bar her way. A man and a woman—both wearing familiar dark blue uniforms and curiously forbidding expressions. Cassie started. Hudson's security staff? What were they doing here and why the hell were they looking at her like that? She felt her mouth grow dry with nameless fear.

'Cassandra Summers?' said one of them.

'Is...something wrong?' she stumbled as the woman took a pen from her pocket and looked Cassie straight in the eye.

'Cassandra Summers? Would you like to come with us?'

'What's happened?' she demanded.

'You have been accused of fraud. And I'm afraid that there's the potential of police involvement—'

'No!' Cassie's denial cut across the official-sounding

words—expecting them to suddenly start laughing. To say that they'd been put up to it by one of her colleagues and that it was nothing more than a practical joke. But their expressions were deadly serious. Staring into their stony faces, she began to tremble uncontrollably as she realised that this was no joke.

'No!' she whispered. 'Please…there must have been some kind of terrible mistake!'

CHAPTER FOUR

GIANCARLO'S cell-phone flashed an incoming call and he frowned when he saw the name which flashed up on the screen.

Cassandra.

His frown deepened. It was barely an hour since he'd seen her and hadn't he said he'd call *her*, even if he hadn't really meant it at the time? Even if just the thought of plunging into that luscious curvy body could send his blood pressure soaring.

But he had been busy appeasing his conscience—telling himself that it would be better for *her* if he just let things drift. Because the last thing an innocent like Cassie needed was to get herself involved with a man with a track record as a heartbreaker. She'd soon be going back home to Cornwall and the Christmas holidays would take her mind off things. And maybe it was better not to get her hopes up by beginning an affair which had no future.

Then snapshot images of blonde hair and pale curves clicked into his memory with aching clarity and, quickly, he lifted the phone.

'Cassandra?' he said, instinctively registering alarm as a barely recognisable voice started pouring out words which made no sense at all. Words like 'fraud' and 'security'. 'Cassandra, is that you? For God's sake—*calm down*! I can't understand a word you're saying. What's going on and where are you?'

'I've been h-hauled off by security staff at the store!' she stumbled. 'They've s-said that I might want to get myself a lawyer.'

'*Lawyer?*' he thundered.

'Yes! There's been the most terrible mix-up—and it's looking serious. Really serious. Giancarlo, r-remember those c-andles you bought...'

He cut right through her blustering hysteria. 'Don't say another word. I'm coming right over,' he said grimly.

His chauffeur drove him straight round to Hudson's, where he demanded to speak to the store manager, who led him to a private room in the bowels of the building where he found Cassie, her face all red and blotchy with tears. A slow fury began to rise inside him as she lifted her face towards his, like a mouse caught in a trap.

'Ah, this must be your lawyer,' said the female security guard, her fingertips automatically touching her hair.

In the midst of her misery, Cassie watched as Giancarlo strode into the room, thinking how strong he looked—and how formidable. Thank God he was here, she thought fervently before blinking in confusion. Her *lawyer*? Her eyes asked him a question but he gave a barely imperceptible shake of his head.

'Hello, Cassandra,' he said. 'Do you want to tell me what's been going on?'

The sound of his voice broke through the emotional barriers she had erected since this whole unbelievable scenario had taken place—an emotional state made more acute by the way she'd spent the previous night. She felt them topple down now, leaving her helpless and vulnerable as she looked up into the obdurate features of his dark face. 'Oh, Giancarlo,' she whispered, tears beginning to slide down her cheeks once more. 'They say I'm a thief!'

Leaning over to press a pristine handkerchief into her palm, Giancarlo turned and fixed the general manager with a blistering look. 'Would you mind telling me what's going on?'

It took only minutes for him to establish that he had not actually paid for the candles he'd bought. He frowned as he tried to remember signing for the impulsive purchase. Maybe he hadn't. The two of them had been too busy flirting and responding to the siren call of their bodies for either of them to notice that his card had not gone through the till.

The problem had been compounded by him forgetting to take the package home with him—and by a rather jealous shop assistant who had set out to cause trouble for Cassandra when she'd seen her in the changing room— only she had really hit the jackpot. On her say-so the floor manager had done a stock-check, discovered the discrepancy, and then immediately alerted the general manager. But the facts were plain enough. The candles had not been paid for and Cassandra had taken them. Technically, there *had* been a theft—and she could be charged.

'*Madre de Dio,*' Giancarlo said beneath his breath— despairing of the chaos which seemed to have come tumbling into his life. How was it possible that a little absent-mindedness could have had such a potentially damaging outcome? Because he had been blinded by her beauty, that was why! Because he, the master of order and control, had acted impulsively—and now he must pay the price for that impulsiveness. And so must she. Her virginity was lost and she was being branded a common thief—oh, she must be delighting in the day that she ever set eyes on him!

But he recognised that anger would not serve him well in such a situation—and neither would sheer force of character. Instead, with the judicious use of tact and determination, he managed to get the matter dropped by explaining that nothing more sinister than a mix-up had occurred and by repaying the money which was still owed.

And fortunately, he was a big-spending customer. He suspected that the jewellery he'd purchased for his various lovers over the years helped ensure that the whole incident was quickly glossed over. Within the hour, he and Cassandra were standing on the pavement outside the glittering windows of the store—while his driver sat in the limousine at the kerbside.

Giancarlo looked down at her slumped and dejected shoulders. 'Are you okay?'

'I'm free, aren't I? If they'd got nasty they might have pressed charges and then I'd have ended up with a criminal record.' She turned her teary eyes up to him—her unlikely saviour. 'Th-thank you,' she said, feeling some of the nightmarish feeling subside—but still unable to shake the strange sensation of numbness. As if everything which had happened since she'd knocked on his front door was happening to somebody else. She swallowed down yet more tears, but her voice was shaking so much that her words stuttered out like little pieces of gravel. 'Th-thank you so much,' she said again, her voice still trembling. 'I feel so st-st-stupid.'

'Well, don't. Don't.' On impulse, he took her into his arms as she began to cry again—feeling her tears soak into his shirt and the soft tremble of her beautiful body as he held her close. And in that moment, her sheer and helpless vulnerability filled him with shame that he should have misjudged her so. Mistaken her for a provocative and experienced lover simply because she had been born to look that way. And now, because of a fierce attraction between them—an attraction which he had seized and capitalised on—her reputation lay in tatters.

Taking his crumpled handkerchief from her trembling fingers, he tilted her chin and began to wipe away the new tears which were trickling down her cheeks. 'Don't blame yourself. It was as much my fault as yours. I wasn't paying attention. Neither of us were.' He looked into her red-rimmed violet eyes and wondered how she could still manage to look so beautiful. 'And you've lost your job.'

'I know.'

'What will you do?'

Cassandra swallowed. In his arms she had felt safe—but now that she was no longer protected by their power-ful warmth the horror of what lay ahead filled her with anxiety. It was more than having to leave Hudson's—though that was bad enough—it was how she was going to explain it to everyone. Her mum. Her flatmates. The owner of the shop back in Padstow when she crept back home and told them all that she had been a failure.

She'd let herself and everyone down—and made her-self look like a complete fool in front of Giancarlo into the bargain. She knew she should be rejoicing that the outcome hadn't been as bad as it could have been—because at least she hadn't acquired a criminal record—but she felt utterly deflated. And isn't part of that because you know that you'll never see him again? Because you've made a fool of yourself in more ways than one.

'I don't know what I'll do,' she whispered. 'But I'll think of something.'

Giancarlo studied the forlorn slant of her shoulders. She was, he realized, still wearing the same dress she'd had on last night—and her face was bleached of all colour and shiny with tears. He felt another sharp stab of conscience.

'Did you have any breakfast this morning?' he demanded.

'Not really. Well, no—I didn't. I was rushing off to work,' said Cassie quickly—not wanting to tell him that the thought of having to face Gina over a coffee-pot had filled her with disquiet.

He glanced at his watch and then pulled open the door of the car, his other hand in the small of her back as he gently propelled her forward. 'Get in.'

'Where are we going?'

'Out for lunch.'

'But I can't go out looking like this.'

'*Precisamente, bella.* That's why we're going shopping first—to buy you something pretty to wear.'

'No, honestly—'

'Yes, *honestly*,' he mocked. 'As a small recompense for the hassle you've had to endure this morning—for which I am partly responsible.'

He made it sound like buying a child an ice cream

after they'd grazed their knee and Cassie flinched. 'I don't want *recompense*!'

'A treat, then. Something nice after something so unpleasant. Please.' He flicked a tear-damp strand of hair away from her lips. 'It will take your mind off things. You know you're going to have to agree, Cassandra—because I won't take no for an answer.'

But something in the way he said it only increased her feelings of unease and isolation. As if she could be bought off—just as he'd bought off the store. Buy her 'something pretty' and she would go away quietly and never bother him again. Well, she would do all that anyway—but without the billionaire pay-off.

'I mean it. I don't want you to buy me something to wear,' she said proudly.

He was about to argue when he saw the fierce light which shone from her eyes and the determined little tilt of her chin and realised that her words were not empty words. And wasn't it a damning indictment of his own life that he should be so taken aback by her rejection of his offer? When had anyone last refused him anything—especially money?

'But I want to take you to lunch,' he persisted softly—because with her spirited little display she had gone from being someone who had the potential to become a burden to an object of desire again. 'Can't I drive you home to change?'

Cassie was about to refuse when something stopped her—because maybe here was an opportunity for them both to get a reality check. Wouldn't Giancarlo be shocked when he realised just how different their two lives were—and wouldn't it help her accept that it would never, ever have worked between them?

'Okay,' she agreed, with a shrug. 'Why not?'

But she felt dry-mouthed and nervous throughout the long ride to Greenford as grand mansions gave way to normal rows of houses and apartment blocks. Because this was where the ordinary people lived—the ones who quietly ran the city. People like her.

When the limousine pulled up outside the apartment block, she could see his eyes narrow slightly and she tried to imagine how it must look to him. There was absolutely nothing wrong with it and seventy people lived within its walls with varying degrees of happiness—but it was like a different world from the rarefied atmosphere of the tree-lined street in which Giancarlo lived.

'Are you going to wait in the car?' she questioned anxiously.

'Why don't I come in?'

What could she say? That she was worried about the inevitable disorder which would greet them—an untidiness caused by too many people living in too small a space? Wouldn't that then seem as if she was *ashamed* of her life, and her friends?

'Please do,' she said, with a forced smile.

It was as bad as she had expected—or, rather, it was worse. Empty beer cans and wine bottles were strewn over the table, along with a few foil containers containing the congealing remains of a curry and—unforgivably— the faint smell of cigarette smoke. Cassie saw Giancarlo give a faint shudder.

'They obviously had some sort of party here!' she said brightly.

'Obviously,' he echoed sardonically.

'Why don't you wait here while I go and get changed? I won't be long.'

'Don't be.'

He watched as she pulled open a bedroom door—glimpsing a room the size of a shoe-box before she closed the door behind her. He thought back to his own days of living frugally—but he had never lived like this. His brilliant law degree had guaranteed that he walked straight into a good job and the power of his personality had meant that he was able to negotiate a good rate on a rented flat where he had lived, while charting his rapid route to success.

The door opened and she emerged. Giancarlo blinked—realising that it was her sheer youth and natural beauty which ensured that in a few moments she had pulled off the kind of look which older, richer women spent all morning in the salon trying to achieve.

She'd put on a simple grey jersey dress and a pair of slouchy black leather boots. She must have quickly washed her face for the smudgy eyes and blotchiness had disappeared—but had added nothing more than a lick of lipstick. Her long pale hair was clipped back at each ear—and the rest fell in a silken tumble around her shoulders. She looked, he thought—utterly delectable.

'Shall we go?' Cassie questioned.

He thought that if she'd been a little more experienced, she might have tried to seduce him here—in an attempt to broker further closeness between them—and the fact that she hadn't tried made him want her. Really want her. He felt the aching at his groin and thought about taking her to bed. Weighed up the novelty and attraction of the idea against the reality of a small and uncomfortable room and the horror of having to be introduced to her flatmates if any of them returned.

'Yes. Let's go,' he answered briskly. 'You must be starving.'

Cassie nodded. At least he hadn't changed his mind about lunch—because hadn't there been a terrible, insecure part of her which had worried that he might have gone by the time she emerged? Simply disappeared, as if he'd thought better of it? She didn't know what she was going to do—but at least this meal could provide a little distraction, which meant she didn't have to think about the future for an hour or so. Her dream of a glorious break in London had now turned into a nightmare. Not only had she been sacked—but she had hitched a star to a thoroughly unsuitable man.

But you haven't hitched your star to him, Cassie, she reminded herself sharply. He's simply taking you for a fancy lunch because you lost your job this morning, and afterwards—he's going to send you on your merry way.

She picked up her handbag. Well, if this was her first and last experience of being Giancarlo's lover, then she was going to enjoy her lunch and not ruin it by moping. She would make the most of it—try to turn the memory into something to be cherished—otherwise, wouldn't it all have been a terrible waste? 'Yes, I'm starving.'

The car drove them to the west of the city, to a restaurant overlooking the river—a big, busy place—so heaven only knew how he managed to get a window table at such short notice. But then Cassie noticed the almost unconscious deference of the waiter—to whom Giancarlo said something smilingly in Italian—and realised that she was in the company of a man who would always get anything he wanted.

She forced herself to concentrate on the green-grey

water of the river as it slid past the window and the
way the intense light reflected back from its rippling
surface—until she was handed a globe of red wine, the
colour of rubies.

'And please don't tell me you never drink at lunch-
time,' said Giancarlo.

'I don't.'

'Well, today you do. You need a drink.' He took a
mouthful of his own, black eyes capturing hers across
the table as he lifted his glass and gave an acid smile.
'Actually, so do I.'

Following his lead, Cassie took a sip and made no
objection when Giancarlo took over the food ordering.
She felt numb—the way your mouth felt when the dentist
gave you an injection. She sat perfectly still as olives and
water and a basket of rosemary-sprinkled bread began
to appear.

'So what will you do?' he questioned, watching her
frozen pose from between narrowed eyes.

'I'll have to go back to Cornwall, I guess.'

'You don't sound keen.'

'I'm not. My mother will want to know why the sudden, rather dramatic change of plan. And so will my
boss.'

'And you won't tell them the truth?'

Cassie gave a hollow laugh. 'What, that I've been
sacked and only just managed to avoid being charged
for theft?'

He raised his eyebrows. 'I suppose when you put it
like that…'

She felt like saying that was the more acceptable of
two explanations—because even worse was the truth
behind her arrest. About not keeping her mind on the

job—swayed by the seasoned charms of an Italian billionaire and then losing her innocence to him. Well, her mother was never going to hear about *that*, either. 'There is no other way to put it.'

'You could stay and get another job,' he suggested.

Cassie shook her head. He just didn't *understand*. But then, why should he—when these sort of commonplace problems were completely outside his experience? 'Three weeks before Christmas?' she questioned. 'I don't think so. Most stores already have their full quota of staff to cope with the holiday rush—and I'm hardly going to be able to dazzle them with a glowing reference.'

Steak and chips were placed in front of them—but Giancarlo scarcely registered one of his favourite dishes. He looked into her eyes, resenting the renewed striking of his conscience provoked by her pale face and troubled expression.

'You could stay anyway—without working,' he suggested.

'I can't stay at the flat without paying rent—it's not fair to the others—and if I'm not working then I can't pay rent. What do they call it—a catch-22 situation?'

He took another mouthful of wine—only now the clarion call of his conscience began to wane as her words took them effortlessly on to more familiar territory. One of funds and finance and supply and demand. Because when he stopped to think about it—didn't they each have something the other wanted? He had the money to cushion her fall from grace—and she had… His eyes drifted over her face.

She had plenty. Violet eyes and soft petal lips and a tight, young body which had caused him to act with such uncharacteristic impulse. He felt the familiar arrowing of desire. Because if he was being honest—he hadn't had enough of Cassandra Summers. And she certainly hadn't had enough of him.

He leaned across the table and took her cold and unresisting hand in his, rubbing his thumb over the pulse, which instantly began to skitter beneath the delicate skin. 'I have a much better idea, *cara*,' he murmured. 'Something which I think could be mutually beneficial to us both.'

Cassie stared at him uncomprehendingly. 'What sort of idea?' she whispered, her senses befuddled just by the way he was touching her.

'Why don't you come and live with me?'

Cassie's heart missed a beat. 'Live with *you*?' she repeated dazedly.

'Mmm.' He saw the flare of hope in her eyes and hurried to make sure she didn't read too much into his suggestion. 'I don't much like the holiday season—but you could provide a very welcome distraction. And in the meantime, you need somewhere to stay.' Giancarlo's lips curved into a sensual smile as he lifted her fingertips and warmed them with the brush of his lips. 'So why don't you come and stay until Christmas?'

CHAPTER FIVE

'What do you mean, you're going to go and live with some bloke you've only just met?'

Gavin's outraged voice made Cassie slowly count to ten as she pulled a dress from the small wardrobe and laid it in her open suitcase. With a smile of confidence she was far from feeling, she turned round to face him.

'For heaven's sake, Gavin,' she chided gently. 'Living in your flat was only ever a temporary stay! I'm twenty-one and this is the twenty-first century—why, in some cultures I'd have been married off at the age of fourteen!'

Gavin's blue eyes bored into hers. 'So he's offering to marry you, is he? This Giancarlo whatever-his-name is?'

'Vellutini. His name's Vellutini,' she said, liking the way her lover's name tasted like velvet on her lips—a soft and sensuous caress, just like his mouth. Until the rest of Gavin's words broke into her daydream and tainted it with the stark edge of reality. 'No, of course he isn't offering to marry me! We've only just met.'

'You've only just met and yet you're moving in with him?'

'So I'm being impulsive!'

'You're being ridiculous.'

'That's your opinion, Gavin—and I don't happen to agree with it.'

'You know he's a billionaire?'

Cassie stared at Gavin, her heart missing a beat. 'I knew he was wealthy—of course I did—but how the hell did you find out a detail like that?'

'Oh, come on, Cassie—don't be so naïve! You think someone like that doesn't have a huge profile on the Internet? I looked him up. He's thirty-five, for heaven's sake—and he's an international playboy! While you're just a sweet, ordinary girl from Cornwall who's batting way, way out of her league.' He glowered. 'A man like that will just chew you up and spit you out when he's finished with you.'

Cassie bit back the indignant retort which flew to her lips, telling herself that Gavin only had her best interests at heart. He'd known her since they'd been at school together and she knew he had feelings for her himself. She'd never encouraged those feelings—but in a way that had only inflamed his protective interest in her. Good-looking himself, in a blond and even-featured kind of way, he had no trouble attracting women—but it was the one who eluded him who held the most allure. Maybe that was the case with all men, thought Cassie with a sudden dejection—remembering the almost indecent haste with which she had accepted Giancarlo's offer to be his mistress. In which case, it didn't hold out much hope for the future.

But she wasn't holding out any hope for the future. She wasn't *completely* stupid. She was simply being a modern woman and taking the relationship for what it was, like lots of women did. Surely that was enough.

'He's my lover,' she told Gavin boldly, because it still sounded like a foreign word. 'Women *do* have lovers, you know. And I'm going to live with him for a few weeks.'

'And then what?'

'Then nothing.' Cassie shrugged with what she hoped was just the right amount of nonchalance. 'I'll be going back to Cornwall to carry on with my life while he carries on with his.'

'You think it'll be that easy, do you?'

'Yes, Gavin,' she said firmly—because deep down Cassie knew that she wanted this far too much to risk listening to the frightened little voice which made her wonder if he was right. 'Actually I do.'

He scowled. 'Well, you know where I am when you need all the pieces picking up.'

It wasn't the blessing she would have chosen but Cassie was determined not to let anything dent her excitement. How could it, when Giancarlo's unbelievable request over lunch had sent her senses into overdrive? And how could she possibly have resisted when he had made the arrangement sound like the perfect solution—and the only sensible option to take? He had leaned across the restaurant table and his ebony gaze had washed over hers, making her feel weak and warm inside and over-whelmed by an irresistible urge to have him kiss her again.

'I am feeling a little guilty, *mia bella*,' he had mur-mured. 'As if I had sat you down for a sumptuous banquet and then whisked you away after the first course. If I'd known that you were inexperienced, I would have—'

He had paused at this point, leaving Cassie to peer at him anxiously. 'Would have what?'

'I made an assumption that there had been other lovers before me,' he said, quickly skating over the question. 'Why wouldn't I have done? A woman of your age is usually experienced. And a man makes love differently if a woman is innocent. The pace is different—and so are his expectations. Your introduction to sex is not what I would have wished—despite the fact that I gave you much pleasure.' Dark eyes had glittered with a message which had made her heart race. 'So come and stay with me and I will show you even more. How does that sound?'

Cassie had blushed. It had sounded like heaven, even when he had said something else—something which would have had any sensible woman running for the hills.

'You know that this—arrangement—is of a purely temporary nature, *bella*? That it ends when it ends—and that means it's over. I need to be honest with you about that.'

Was that honesty or was it cruelty? Cassie didn't care. She could handle it because she wanted him far too much to listen to the voice of reason. As she hugged Gavin goodbye and ran outside her Greenford flat to find Giancarlo's car sitting purring at the kerbside she couldn't quell a great surge of exhilaration. Because this was the most exciting thing to have ever happened to her and she was going to enjoy every second of it.

Ignoring the nagging little voice which questioned whether this was going to be a romantic high-point from which she would never recover, Cassie settled back in the car as she was driven to Giancarlo's house.

The door was opened by Gina, a careful smile on her face—her expression impossible to read behind the trendy, black-framed spectacles.

'Hello, Cassandra,' she said. 'I understand that I am to welcome you. Giancarlo won't be back from the office until six—but he said you were to settle yourself in. Shall I show you to your dressing room—so that you can unpack—or would you prefer me to do that for you?'

Cassie hesitated. Gina didn't sound at all fazed by the fact that a stranger was moving into her well-ordered house. Did she have to cope with this scenario on a regular basis? she wondered. And the last thing she wanted was the elegant housekeeper giving her rather humble clothes the once-over. But she hid all her misgivings behind an equally careful smile. 'Thanks—but I can unpack myself.'

She followed Gina upstairs to a previously unseen room which led directly off the master bedroom—one containing shelves, cupboards, floor-length mirrors and another swish en-suite bathroom. It was ridiculously large for her meagre amount of belongings but, once Gina had gone, she unpacked. And once she'd put away her few bits and pieces and placed a framed photo of her parents on the window sill it felt a lot more like home.

Six o' clock seemed like ages away and she took a long bath and washed her hair, luxuriating in the scent-filled steam from the bathroom, and was just sitting wrapped in a towel in front of the dressing table when the door opened—and in walked Giancarlo.

It was the first time she'd seen him since lunch yesterday—and her heart began to pound with a trembling kind of excitement as she turned round to find his gaze raking over her. For a moment he didn't say anything—just

studied her from between narrowed eyes—and Cassie
sat frozen like a statue. What if he was now regretting
his decision—if the reality of coming home and finding
her in situ was threatening his bachelor independence?

She swallowed. Say something. Don't just sit there.
'H-hello.'

Once more he allowed his eyes to rake over her—at
the soft white towel covering her pink-flushed skin and
her hair trailing in damp tendrils all the way down her
back. He had been distracted all day—wondering if he
had taken leave of his senses in giving her access to his
house—before reminding himself that she had nowhere
else to go. But now that he had seen her again, his res-
ervations dissolved. God, she was beautiful.

The swift and heady rush of desire heated his veins as
he walked towards her and repeated her trembled little
greeting, and yet something in her big violet eyes made
his voice gentle as he leaned over her. 'Hello,' he said as
he bent his head to whisper a kiss on her bare shoulder.
'Is this the way you're always going to greet me when I
get home from work?'

'Do you like it?' she whispered, closing her eyes as
she felt the soft, seductive graze of lips.

'Yes, I think we can safely say that I like it, *cara*. I
like it very much. Though I think we could improve on
it even more.' His hand moved round to give a little tug
of the knot which constrained the towel so that it fell
away—revealing her rosy-tipped breasts, the slender dip
of her waist and the rounded curve of her pale hips. She
looked like a still-life painting come to glorious life, he
thought as he let his fingers drift downwards to cup one
breast.

Cassie's eyes opened wide as she saw the image

reflected back from the mirror—his olive fingers contrasted against the paleness of her own skin. She could feel the insistent peaking of her nipple against his palm and the warm heat in the pit of her stomach as his lips grazed over her damp hair. Restlessly, she wriggled—tried to turn to have him kiss her properly—but he wouldn't let her. 'Giancarlo,' she breathed.

'Stay,' he commanded as his fingers continued to stroke her.

'But it's—'

'Stay!'

Despite her erotic imprisonment, she felt a hot, fierce heat shoring up inside her—building and building as he reached further down, his fingers tangling in the soft fuzz of hair at the juncture of her thighs and the honeyed moistness it concealed. She squirmed as he moved against her heated flesh and gasped his name as she felt the heat now spiralling upwards—like a great, strong tidal wave which was carrying her in its rush. It had happened to her when he had taken her to bed—but he had been there with her, not fully dressed like this, as if she were some kind of erotic puppet and he were pulling the strings. As if he were not part of what was happening to her. But then those new and extraordinary sensations began to engulf everything else—so that the world seemed to be composed of nothing other than sheer delight.

'Giancarlo,' she gasped, closing her eyes as she felt it about to happen.

'No, watch,' he urged. 'Watch yourself in the mirror, *mia bella*. Watch how beautiful you look when you experience pleasure.'

Obediently, Cassie's lids fluttered open to see that

her eyes were dark with desire. Glancing upwards, she met his mocking reflection in the mirror—felt control slipping away as his fingers continued their insistent dance. And then desire dissolved within her—leaving her helpless to do anything but watch herself orgasm. She saw the involuntary jerk of her body and the way that the high colour in her cheeks seemed to spread all over her breasts—as if someone had washed them in rose-pink paint.

Weakly, she clutched onto his arm until the spasms had died away—feeling as if she might float away if she let go of him—but now Giancarlo had moved forward and he lifted her up into his arms. And she thought how decadent it seemed that he was still in his work suit while she was completely naked.

'Wasn't that the most erotic thing imaginable?' he murmured, pressing his lips over hers and feeling her warm sensuality rising up to meet him.

Still dazed, Cassie nodded—because she couldn't deny his words. It was. But as he took her through into the bedroom she thought that it had been...been....

What?

A demonstration of his superior sexuality. A pleasure-fest, yes—but without any of the attendant romance of deep kisses and tender caresses that her foolish heart had craved. Did he sense her misgivings? Was that why he sat her down on the edge of the bed and crouched in front of her?

'Are you going to undo my tie?' he murmured.

With trembling fingers, she complied—realising that he meant her to carry on, so she unbuttoned the silk shirt, too. He helped her with the belt and the trousers, swiftly divesting himself of the rest of his clothes until he was as naked as she, his body all satin-sheened skin and powerful limbs.

'Oh, Giancarlo,' she whispered as she felt the hard length of his arousal pressing insistently against her.

'What?'

'I didn't realise—'

'That it could be so good?' His lips curved into a smile before drifting to her neck. 'And I didn't realise that you would be so beautifully responsive. So quick to orgasm and so eager to learn.'

He pushed her back onto the bed and moved over her, his fingers entwining in the spill of her hair and his lips whispering over hers in tantalising little kisses. And Cassie revelled in the growing familiarity of his body. Already, she was eager to reacquaint herself with the feel of tensile muscle beneath the silken skin and the honed perfection of his torso. This time she knew exactly when he wanted her to part her legs—and although she knew now what to expect, the glorious intimacy of his first thrust still took her breath away.

Glancing up, she could see that the ebony eyes were slitted and opaque as he entered her, could see the play of muscles in his powerful shoulders as he moved inside her. His lips dipped to tease hers—brushing and biting and grazing—until she greedily raised her hands to pull his head down, hearing his soft laugh as he deepened the kiss. She revelled in the changing rhythm—the way his hands clamped around her waist so that he could draw her even closer—until she felt so full of him that there was only one way to release herself from this exquisite tension and that was to let go.

She cried out—a strange, broken little sound she scarcely recognised as her own voice—and almost immediately she heard his own ragged groan. Afterwards, she lay there for a warm age, wrapped in his arms—her head on his chest as she listened to the thundering of his heart as it grew steady and his hand stroked absently at her hair.

But Cassie felt shaken as she lay in the curve of his arms. She hadn't realised that sex could make you feel so utterly vulnerable—even more vulnerable than she'd felt in that room with the security officers at Hudson's. Or that it could bind you to a man—make you want to cling to him and never let him go.

He must have gone to sleep, for his hand stilled to lie on top of her head, and she risked turning slightly, her eyes drinking in the details of his face as if she was committing them to memory.

In sleep the rugged features were relaxed—his expression less stern. She studied the dark sweep of his lashes and the way his hard mouth had softened into a sensual pout. It suddenly occurred to her that the man he really was lay concealed behind the rather formidable mask he always wore. Would he ever let her see what lay beneath?

She was unprepared for his sudden awakening—the way those lashes parted to reveal the ebony gleam beneath.

Giancarlo stretched and gave a lazy yawn. *'Eri persa nei tuoi pensieri,'* he murmured.

She pleated her brows in response. 'What does that mean?'

'That your thoughts were elsewhere.'

Cassie pushed the hair back off her face. 'They were.'

'Usually a danger sign where a woman is concerned,' he observed drily.

'I was thinking…' She hesitated, because despite the intimacies they'd just shared there was something still a little intimidating about him. 'That I don't really know anything about you,' she finished softly.

His index finger stroked from neck to nipple, his mouth curving as he registered her answering shiver. 'Yes, you do,' he contradicted silkily. 'You know how to turn me on with your big violet eyes and your petal lips and your soft, firm curves. You're learning a little more every time we make love. By the time you go home to Cornwall, you will have become a sleek and seasoned lover who will be able to captivate any man you choose.'

Cassie supposed that was a kind of compliment— the kind of thing a man *would* say to his temporary mistress—but it made her feel like nothing more than a body. Somebody without a mind of her own. 'But I don't know anything about your life, Giancarlo.'

Giancarlo let his hand drift down to her breast. Why did women always want to interrogate you—and at the most inappropriate times? Hadn't he hoped that his little shop-girl would be docile when he wanted her to be? He sighed. 'What do you want to know?'

'Tell me how you ended up living in London.'

'It's a long story.'

'Those are the best ones.'

In spite of himself, he smiled—his finger stilling on the puckering rosy flesh of her nipple. 'You are very persistent, aren't you?'

She bit her lip as she felt pleasure rippling from where

he was touching her. Was he trying to distract her? 'J-just interested.'

He looked into her flushed face. 'I told you that I was Tuscan by birth?'

'Mmm.' Cassie nodded, snuggling a little closer to him. 'What's it like in Tuscany?'

The clean, fresh smell of her struck some long-hidden chord within him so that for once he allowed himself to think of the green hills and sun-washed landscape of home—even though he had ring-fenced his memories and put them out of bounds. Exiled himself from it in all the ways that he could—so that even on his rare, duty visits home he didn't allow nostalgia or sentiment to lure him.

'What's it like? Well, it is very beautiful. In fact, some people say it's the most beautiful place on earth.'

'So why…why live here, and not there?'

'It's complicated.' He wound a strand of blonde hair around his finger. 'My brother lives there—and it's a little too small for both of us.'

He had a brother. She felt as if she had just discovered a missing piece of a jigsaw puzzle. 'What's he like?'

'We're twins.'

'Twins!' She turned onto her tummy and looked at him. 'Identical twins?'

'Not really. Well, we…look the same,' he said, and then gave a short laugh. 'But no two men are identical, Cassandra—if you were a little more experienced, you'd know that.'

Cassie registered the darkness which underpinned his voice. 'You had some sort of fall-out?' she guessed softly.

Giancarlo looked into her eyes and suddenly had the

strangest desire to tell her. Was it because pillow talk and secrets were the currency traditionally shared with a mistress—or because her place in his life was so temporary that telling her would have no impact on it? She didn't mix in his circles and she never would. And hadn't he buried the memory so deep that he was curious now to see what it would look like if he dragged it out into the cold and dispassionate light of day?

'A fall-out? Yes, I guess you could say that.'

'What happened?'

Giancarlo swallowed because the acid taste of betrayal could still catch him unawares. Even now. He stared at the ceiling. 'It all started soon after the death of our parents. My mother died when I was twelve—my father five years earlier.'

'That must have been very hard,' said Cassie softly.

She had the kind of voice which soothed—which felt like balm on his troubled recall. 'Yes. It was a lonely kind of childhood. Plenty of money but not much else.'

'And who looked after you?'

'Oh, we had a series of guardians—aristocratic and intellectual men appointed by the estate who were supposed to educate us, and who we used to take pleasure in outwitting.' He shrugged his broad, naked shoulders. 'We were pretty much a law unto ourselves. And of course—we were fiercely competitive. Life was a constant battle to each prove ourselves—maybe to compensate for the lack of parental guidance.'

His mouth hardened. And the lack of warmth, or softness, of course—for there had been no compensatory woman's touch. No comfort or reassurance from the gentler sex given to two little rich boys who ran wild as gypsies.

Giancarlo felt something like pain as memories came flooding back—more vivid than he had expected them to be. 'Both Raul and I went to university in Rome. I read law and he read business. We were due to inherit the family estate when we turned twenty-one and we were going to work it between us.'

He remembered Gabriella, too. Tiny and beautiful—with thick hair even blacker than his own and eyes like polished jet. Gabriella, the darling and beauty of the campus. The woman every man had wanted and she had wanted Giancarlo. Oh, yes. His competitive nature had been at first flattered and then seduced by her attention towards him. How he had basked in her adoration and the envy of his peers and how he had revelled in that hot, heady explosion of first love. For a while they became the golden couple—making plans for the future and the family they would make together. And then...

'So what happened?'

Cassie's question broke into his thoughts. 'We both qualified.'

'Similar degrees?'

'Mine was better.' He shrugged. 'And that is not a boast, but a fact. And that rankled with my brother. On our twenty-first birthday we were summoned into our lawyer's office and told that Raul would inherit everything. The farms. The vineyards. The olive groves and the properties in Rome and Siena. The vast estates with which the Vellutini name was synonymous would all pass to him.' He paused. 'While I would receive precisely nothing.'

Cassie stiffened as she heard the cold note which had entered his voice. 'Nothing?' she echoed, bewildered.

'*Niente,*' he confirmed and then emphasised the word again in English. 'Nothing.'

'But that's terrible! *Why?*'

Giancarlo knew then why he had buried the story. The words were still like bitter poison to say and the betrayal they evoked more bitter still. 'Because we had been born by Caesarean section and Raul was plucked from our mother's womb exactly two minutes before me.' His voice roughened. 'Making him the true heir to the Vellutini fortune.'

'I can't believe it,' Cassie breathed as she stared into the black brilliance of his eyes. 'That's...unbelievable!'

'Have you never heard about primogeniture?' he questioned softly. 'The first-born's right of inheritance. It's pretty feudal—some might say primitive—but legally binding, all the same.'

She let the words sink in, trying to imagine what she might have done if she'd been in his brother's position. 'But didn't...Raul—feel morally obliged to share some of his good fortune with you?'

Giancarlo's lips curved into an acid smile as he remembered the look of unmistakable delight on his brother's face—and the subsequent and insulting offer of a small, barren piece of land in Puglia, which he had rejected. 'Not in any real sense, no. Sharing wasn't really Raul's thing. In fact, in the true spirit of sibling rivalry—and maybe to make up for all the times I'd beaten him—he decided that he still hadn't got quite enough. So for good measure he also took Gabriella, the woman I was going to marry—although, to be fair, he didn't have to try very hard. She liked the finer things in life and Raul was able to provide them for her. Why hang around with the twin who was going to have to work for his living when you could lead a life of luxury as a rich man's wife?'

Cassie bit back a gasp as she thought about the impact that must have had on him. Why, it must have been like a kick in the teeth—no money and, then, no girlfriend. His imagined future completely distorted. His pride trampled underfoot. And that might hit him harder than anything else, she realised—with a sudden flash of insight. 'So what happened?'

'I came to England and worked for a law firm which specialised in Italian property deals. There weren't many people in that field at the time and so I was in a strong position. At first I lived frugally, and worked hard—a habit which I've never quite lost. With the money I saved and the insider knowledge I gained I was eventually able to start buying property myself. And I was rather good at it—or, rather, I had a talent for spotting places ahead of the market. I bought in down-town New York before it became the fashionable thing to do. I speculated in areas of London which popular thinking said would never take off—but which soared. Buy low and sell high—it's not an original concept, but that doesn't mean it doesn't work. It's how I built up my business into what it is today.'

Cassie thought how animated his face had become as he'd talked about his business—it had been the most alive she'd seen it apart from when he was making love to her. She could see that it must have mended his wounded pride and brought him immense satisfaction to make money for himself, rather than having it easy by inheriting it. But Cassie's question hadn't really been about the money. She had been far more interested in the other part of the betrayal.

'And what about your ex-girlfriend?' she questioned carefully. 'What happened to her?'

'Gabriella? Oh, she married my brother and they're still together. In fact, they have a daughter and are living on the family estate.'

Cassie stared into his face, searching for clues about how he felt but there was nothing other than the little flicker of a pulse at his temple and his voice sounded completely casual. Almost too casual. Did he still hanker after the woman who had betrayed him? she wondered. And was that betrayal the reason why he had never married—why a man as gorgeous as he was should live a life which seemed essentially lonely at its heart?

'Oh, Giancarlo,' she whispered. 'I'm so sorry.'

At her unasked-for words of sympathy Giancarlo stilled, wondering why he had said so much—and *why to her*? Because she had that cute little way of asking—of widening her violet eyes—so that uncharacteristically he had found himself telling her? His mouth hardened. Well, she need not imagine that this was the first of many confidences he would share with her—or that she had found the key to 'understanding' him. He would tell her the truth and, although it might hurt her a little now, it would warn her off amassing much greater hurt in the future.

'Please don't waste your sorrow on me, Cassandra,' he advised softly. 'Don't they say that it is hardship which hones the character? And can't you see that it is immensely more satisfying to have made my own fortune than to have it bestowed on me by an accident of birth?'

'I wasn't thinking about…about the money,' Cassie said hesitantly. 'But more about your girlfriend.'

Did she really imagine that he was still carrying a torch for the woman who had been nothing but an out-and-out gold-digger—someone who could be bought by the highest bidder? 'Again, your sentiments are misplaced, Cassandra,' he said silkily, his eyes glittering out a distinct warning. 'You see, in many ways she did me a big favour. It taught me early in life the valuable lesson of never trusting a woman.'

CHAPTER SIX

'What is that *monstrosity* hanging on the front door?'

Cassie waited until Giancarlo had put his briefcase down in the hall before drawing a deep breath. 'It's a Christmas wreath.'

He turned to her, his eyes narrowed. 'Forgive me, I phrased myself badly, *bella*. I know exactly what it is. I meant—what the hell is it doing there?'

'I thought it looked…pretty.'

'And I thought I told you that I don't do Christmas.'

Cassie swallowed. 'I know you did—I just don't understand why.'

'Because it's nothing but misrepresentation. It allows sentiment to masquerade as emotion, depicts unrealistically happy families and dresses up greed as some sort of seasonal need.'

'Bah-humbug!'

His eyes narrowed. 'Excuse me?'

'It's a joke. Something you say about people who don't like Christmas. People like you.'

'I think you're missing the point, *cara*. When I say that I don't like Christmas it means you should heed my words—not attempt to change my mind. Especially after a long day at work when I want to be greeted with nothing more controversial than a kiss.'

Cassie moved into his arms. 'No, I suppose not.'

Giancarlo saw that her lips had softened just the way they always did when he was about to kiss her—but he heard the unmistakable trace of defiance in her soft voice. 'And anyway, where did you get the money to buy such a magnificent monstrosity—when you have refused point-blank to accept any funds from me?' Her stubborn refusal to do so had at first made him suspicious—for he couldn't believe that there was a woman alive who wouldn't itch to be given free use of his credit card during her tenure as his mistress.

He had tried insisting that she would *need* money—in order to go shopping. And that was when she had told him that she had no intention of doing anything as dull as shopping while she was installed in his London town house. That she could go shopping any time and she wasn't particularly into consumerism. He remembered his surprise when he realised that she actually meant it. And that she intended spending her days enjoying the city for free—by visiting the many galleries and parks the capital had to offer.

But now it seemed that Cassandra—who would sigh wistfully whenever they passed a tacky Christmas window display—had finally succumbed and given into the temptation of a seasonal wreath.

'I made it,' she said suddenly as his lips brushed against hers.

'Made what?'

'The wreath.'

'You can't have *made* it. It looks far too professional.'

'But I *did*, Giancarlo—we do sell crafts in our shop, you know, and we are supposed to know something about them. I found a sweet park-keeper in Kensington Gardens, who let me pick some holly and ivy—and I asked your driver if he had any wire I could use. And then I found the base in a cheap little—'

'Enough!' protested Giancarlo, but for a moment he was laughing as he bent his lips to her ear. 'I had no idea that my mistress could be so damned stubborn.'

'Didn't you?' she questioned, winding her arms around his neck. She was about to tease him back—to say something on the lines of, *Well, maybe you have a lot to learn, Giancarlo.* Except that wouldn't be true. He didn't want to learn anything about *her*, not really—and even if he did, there was no time left in which to do it.

The hours had become days and the days had become weeks—and there were only a few days before their arrangement came to an end. Five days until Christmas Eve—when she would be dispatched back to Cornwall like a parcel which had just caught the last post.

And her time with Giancarlo would be over for ever.

She tried not to dwell on it—to think instead of the pleasure she had had with him. All the shows, the films and the dinners they had shared—and her glorious and continuing education in the joys of sex, taught by a true master of the art. It had been just the two of them—as if the rest of the world didn't matter—isolated in their own erotic little bubble.

And all the while she had been trying not to focus on the time which was draining away and bringing the day of her departure closer and closer—but it wasn't easy. Especially not when you had started to care for a man who had tacitly warned you that to care for him would be a complete waste of time. But the human heart was stubbornly impervious to reason, or warnings. Sometimes it made you long for the things you could never have...

She broke away from his kiss and looked up at him. 'So can we keep the wreath?'

'That depends.'

'On what?'

His lips curved into a smile as his fingers squeezed at one pert globe of her delectable bottom. 'On what you are prepared to do to make me agreeable.'

Glad that they had the house to themselves, Cassie slid her hand down over his belly and laid the palm of her hand over his groin. Through the immaculate suit trousers, she could feel his unmistakable arousal pressing against her. And as she stroked him with growing insistence through the fine material she lifted her lips to touch the faint rasp of his jaw.

'Why don't you come upstairs and find out?'

'Or why don't we find out right here?' he growled.

She needed no second bidding, revelling in his powerless capitulation as she unzipped and then slithered down his trousers and slid to her knees in front of him. She took him in her lips—savouring the silken steel of his shaft, teasing it with the soft flick of her tongue and then sliding it deep inside her mouth so that he gasped. Holding onto his hips, she kept up the seductive rhythm while he feverishly tangled his fingers in her hair and then she felt the tension build—heard his helpless groan as he could contain himself no longer. And she felt an odd sense of triumph as he began to spill his seed inside her mouth.

Afterwards, there was silence for a moment—punctuated

only by the sound of Giancarlo frantically drawing air back into his lungs. Then slowly, he brought her up to standing, his eyes almost opaque with lust as they scanned her face. Touching his finger to her lips, he bent his head to kiss her—tasting his own essential scent on her skin.

'Let's go to bed,' he said softly.

'Yes, please,' she whispered.

In the bedroom, he removed her clothes so slowly and erotically that she writhed beneath his fingers, her blood on fire. His own clothes he took off much more efficiently, his eyes not leaving hers as his silk shirt fluttered to the floor like a flag of surrender. And at last the dark boxers were removed, to reveal his tumescent arousal in all its magnificent glory.

'You look daunted, *cara*,' he murmured.

She glanced at him from beneath her lashes. 'Is it… is it normal for a man to be as aroused as often as you are, Giancarlo?'

He gave a low laugh tinged with satisfaction as he began to stroke her—and yet, in truth, her eagerness and her appreciation were a constant aphrodisiac which never failed to arouse him. 'You will find few men to match me in terms of libido, *bella*.'

She supposed it was her own fault for asking, but his matter-of-fact reply sent a faint tremor through her body—making her feel as if she were nothing but another notch on his bedpost.

But she was just a notch, wasn't she? Giancarlo had never promised her anything else—so if she found the thought of saying goodbye to him unpalatable, then she had only herself to blame.

Yet all her doubts and her anxieties were dissolved when his hands moved over her with practised ease.

He stroked her quivering skin until she was a mass of sensitive nerve-endings and she moaned his name softly beneath her breath as he brought her slowly down onto his aching shaft.

'Giancarlo,' she breathed.

'Look at me,' he instructed silkily.

Their eyes locked as he guided her hips into a deep rhythm and his captured gaze when he was deep inside her seemed unbearably intimate. But as the erotic dance led her inexorably towards orgasm she shut her eyes tightly again—afraid that he would see the naked pain which sometimes intruded at the very moment of pleasure. Pain provoked by the thought of a life without him.

It was only later, when they were showered and dressed and eating a delicious dinner cooked by Gina—who had returned from her shopping trip—that Giancarlo raised his glass to her in silent toast.

'Tell me, *bella mia*,' he said softly. 'Do you have a passport?'

The unexpected question made Cassie put down her wine glass as she looked at him—her heart thudding as she basked in the ebony stare he was slanting at her.

'Yes. Yes—of course I have a passport.'

'No "of course" about it,' he pointed out, with a dry smile. 'Since you told me you'd never been to Europe.'

'Ah, but I went on a day trip to Calais when I was at school—does that count?'

Giancarlo bit back an indulgent smile as she pushed away her plate and looked at him with interest. As a mistress she had been perfect. Unwittingly amusing. Sexually curious—and with a native intelligence which sometimes surprised him. He had enjoyed introducing her to theatre and the opera—even if he hadn't got round to introducing her to his friends. Why bother, when she would never encounter them again? No, early on he'd realised that time spent with Cassandra could be spent in a much more enjoyable way than sitting through interminable dinner parties and fielding off faintly embarrassing questions about how they'd met.

But while shaving that morning he had realised with something of a shock that there was hardly any time left and that Christmas was almost upon them. For once, he had not noticed the passing days nor been bored by the constant company of one woman. Barely a week to go until he travelled to New York to spend the holidays with friends—the way he always did. And when he returned to London it would be to a bed and a life bereft of his young, blonde lover.

Would he miss her?

He studied her as the tip of her little pink tongue snaked its way around her lips to make them gleam provocatively. And he remembered what that same talented little tongue had been doing just a little while ago. For a woman who had known nothing of a man's body when he had first met her, she had proved to be a remarkably quick and talented learner.

Yes, he would miss her—but he would soon forget her. He always did.

'Oh, I can think of more enjoyable ways of seeing the Continent than a school day trip,' he murmured.

'Really?'

'How would you like to go to Paris?' he asked suddenly.

'Paris?' she squeaked.

'Capital of France,' he said gravely. 'Have you heard of it?'

Cassie looked into the gleam of his black eyes—at the rugged, proud features which made her heart flip every time he came into the room. 'Oh, Giancarlo—do you really mean it?'

'I really do.'

'When?'

'How would tomorrow morning suit you?'

'That soon? Oh, my goodness! Yes, please. Oh—thank you! *Thank you!*' She jumped up from her seat and slid her arms tightly around his neck just as Gina walked into the room to collect the plates. Quickly, Cassie let her arms fall—even if she hadn't felt the sudden tensing of Giancarlo's shoulders. Because he didn't do demonstrative—not in the street, not in restaurants or in the theatre, and he certainly didn't do demonstrative in front of his cool housekeeper.

Getting used to having live-in staff had proved more challenging than learning to share a bed. Gina hadn't been *unfriendly* towards Cassie—she had just showed a polite indifference which could be terribly intimidating at times. And while Cassie could see that Giancarlo needed people to run his house for him, she wished that they could have all been dismissed during her brief stay there. She would have liked to have had the freedom to roam the house. To make love in every room. To cook for him herself instead of always having their meals served up to them—either at home or in some fancy restaurant. Because she wasn't interested in all the trappings which came with Giancarlo's great wealth—she was interested in *him*.

'Cassandra and I are going to Paris for a few days,'

said Giancarlo as a pink-cheeked Cassie returned to her seat.

'How delightful,' said Gina, with a cool smile. 'Paris is always lovely at this time of year.'

Cassie gave a watery kind of smile, thinking that the whole world was more well travelled than she was! But she blotted out her insecurity as she got ready for the trip. A few weeks ago, packing for such an event would have been beset with problems, but not any more—mainly because her wardrobe had expanded slightly to accommodate her role as a tycoon's mistress. It had started when Giancarlo had returned from work late one night bearing two fancy carrier bags—both festooned with soft layers of tissue paper. Cassie recognised the brand names immediately and blinked as he handed them to her.

'What are these?'

'Why don't you open them and find out?'

From the first bag she pulled out a black silk dress which slithered through her fingers like a snake. 'Oh!'

'Like it?'

'How could I not like it? It's…it's…*beautiful*. But how did you know my size?'

There was a pause. A smile. A shrug. And Cassie's cheeks grew hot with embarrassment as she correctly read the expression in his eyes. Of course. She wasn't the first woman he had bought clothes for and she certainly wouldn't be the last. He was *an expert* in guessing a woman's size.

Her fingers were trembling as she opened the second bag, which contained a pair of shoes—a pair as high as the ones she'd worn on their first date, but there all similarity ended. These were pure leather, handmade and exquisitely crafted, with a band of tiny glass beads at the toe which made them look as if they'd been dipped in fairy dust. In fact, they were fairytale shoes for a fantasy world—and a sudden sense of unreality washed over her.

'What are these for?' she breathed.

'For wearing, of course.'

Cassie's heart started beating very fast. 'Because my own clothes aren't good enough, I suppose?'

'Oh, come on—don't take it so personally. Showering mistresses with expensive gifts is written in the contract, Cassandra,' he said softly. 'Didn't you know that?'

She could have flung the shoes back at him—except that it would have achieved precisely nothing. It was pointless issuing ultimatums or sulking simply because he wouldn't behave in the way she would have secretly liked him to behave—like a man who was falling in love. Because Giancarlo would never do that. He treated her like a mistress because she *was* a mistress. And if she had found herself wanting the relationship to deepen instead of coming to an abrupt end—well, then she was wasting her time.

Because that was never going to happen. It had never been part of the deal. And if she had been grown-up enough to accept his terms from the outset, then she should be grown-up enough not to want to move the goalposts because she'd discovered that it didn't really suit her after all. So she accepted his gifts with a kind of calm emptiness—and found that when it came to visiting the most romantic capital in the world she had the perfect wardrobe to take with her.

She had thought they might fly, but instead they took the train—a champagne trip through the Channel

FREE BOOKS OFFER

To get you started, we'll send you
2 FREE books and a FREE gift

There's no catch, everything is **FREE**

Accepting your 2 **FREE** books and **FREE** mystery gift
places you under no obligation to buy anything.

Be part of the Mills & Boon® Book Club™ and receive your favourite
Series books up to 2 months before they are in the shops and delivered
straight to your door. Plus, enjoy a wide range of **EXCLUSIVE** benefits!

Best new women's fiction – delivered right to
your door with FREE P&P

Avoid disappointment – get your books up to
2 months before they are in the shops

No contract – no obligation to buy

2 **FREE** books
and a
FREE gift

We hope that after receiving your free books you'll
want to remain a member. But the choice is yours.
So why not give us a go? You'll be glad you did!

Visit **millsandboon.co.uk** to stay up to date
with offers and to sign-up for our newsletter

Tunnel, emerging from the darkness into the flat, French countryside until the train drew into Paris, at the Gare du Nord.

'Are you ready for Christmas?' questioned Giancarlo as he ushered her through the station to where a car was waiting for them. 'Because this city does it better than any other.'

Cassie nodded as she climbed into the luxurious leather interior of the limousine, feeling as excited as a small child who had been told she was going to meet Father Christmas. 'Ready for anything,' she whispered.

Fairy lights woven into the trees gleamed golden-bright all the way along the Champs Élysées, and Christmas trees were festooned with fake snow. Cassie sat very close to him in the back of the car as they passed all the famous designer stores—Chanel, Gucci and Louis Vuitton—with their clever-clever windows and pencil-thin mannequins.

They were staying at a grand hotel not far from the Eiffel Tower—with a foyer in which stood the biggest Christmas tree Cassie had ever seen. It was looped with lights and hung with cinnamon sticks and baubles which glittered like icicles—and beneath it were stacked piles of fake, gold-wrapped presents.

Giancarlo had rented an enormous suite whose huge windows overlooked the Avenue Montagne where champagne awaited them—as well as big vases of bright pink roses. The bed was indescribably opulent and one of the two bathrooms contained a Jacuzzi. For a while Cassie wandered around like a woman in a trance as her fingertips skated over the heavy brocade arm of an antique sofa.

'I keep thinking that this is a dream and that soon I will wake up.'

'Well, don't go to sleep just yet,' he murmured as he pulled her into his arms. 'Didn't you know that Paris was invented for lovers?'

For a moment the word mocked her. *Lovers*, he had said—but it was an intensely misleading word, because what did this have to do with love? And how many other of his lovers had he brought to this romantic city?

But Cassie pushed the nagging thought away as Giancarlo began to undress her, sliding the whisper-soft silk lingerie from her trembling flesh as his mouth found her breast.

For three days they did all the things which tourists were supposed to do—climbing up the Eiffel Tower and marvelling at all the cathedrals and beautiful little churches which studded the city. Exploring the tiny side streets, they discovered dusty antique shops in which to browse. They walked through a frosty Left Bank and ate *boeuf bourguignon* with crusty bread and on another day they wandered through the Tuileries Gardens and watched the ever-changing light reflected on the river Seine. And when they weren't exploring they were having sex—amazing sex, which Cassie suspected was sharpened by the sense that it would all soon be over.

But that sense of displacement never quite left her—and it was reinforced on their last day, when he tried to buy her a beautiful black suede coat which he'd seen in the window of Valentino and persuaded her to try on.

She shook her head. 'Thank you—but no.'

'But I want you to have it, *bella*,' he said, in a voice of silky determination.

'No, Giancarlo,' said Cassie firmly, even though she

could barely recognise the sleek, *chic* woman who stared back at her from the mirror.

'Why not?'

'Because...because it's so *expensive*.'

'Well, why not? You're worth it...'

'No!' she said fiercely, her cheeks growing pink. 'Please don't say that. It makes me feel like some kind of...of...*commodity*.'

There was a pause. 'If you're trying to make me feel bad, then let me warn you now that you won't succeed,' he drawled, but Cassie couldn't mistake the irritation which underpinned his words.

In the brightly lit shop their eyes clashed and one word leapt to the forefront of Cassie's mind, while nearby the sales assistant pretended not to notice.

'*Warn* me?'

'Just don't bother trying to lay a guilt trip on me, *bella*. It's coming to the end of our time together and I wanted to buy you a warm coat, that's all. I've noticed you don't have one—and there's a long, cold winter ahead.'

Cassie stared at him, feeling sick. He was making her sound like some urchin from a Victorian melodrama—standing in a threadbare coat selling matches while snowflakes swirled down around her!

'You know what you can do with your damned coat,' she flared as she pulled it off and thrust it at him. And, turning round, she walked out of the shop without looking back.

He caught up with her outside and his face was dark with fury as he caught hold of her, his fingers biting into the thin material of her coat, which now seemed to mock her. 'Don't *ever* do that again,' he snapped.

'What, refuse to be bought off?'

'I'm talking about making a scene in public. Do you think I don't care about my reputation—even if you have no regard for your own?'

Her body beginning to tremble, Cassie stared at him. And as his critical words registered the scales began to fall from her eyes. How could she have been so *stupid*? Just because she had allowed herself to be completely captivated by his magnetism and charm, she had credited him as having all kinds of attributes which didn't exist outside her wistful imagination.

Because to Giancarlo she *was* a commodity. She was his mistress and he paid the bills. He brought her to Paris and in return she provided sex on tap. It was temporary and it meant nothing. *Nothing.*

He had spoken of reputation, but he had missed the point somewhere along the way. Because with one stroke he had managed to both save and ruin *her* reputation. Yes, he had ensured she didn't have to return to Cornwall after being sacked for suspected theft—but he had persuaded her to enter into a liaison which made a mockery of all the things she believed in. Her idealistic dreams of love and fidelity had been smashed.

She had learnt that if a woman provided good sex to a rich man she was rewarded with clothes costing tens of thousands of pounds. That had been the price she'd been paid for the loss of her innocence—and maybe the cost was too high. An adventure in London had become nothing but a sordid affair—and the sooner she left it all behind, the better.

But afterwards she half wished that she had just gone ahead and let him buy her the coat because it ruined the rest of the trip—and, in a way, it ruined their goodbye.

Countless times she had played out in her head what

he might say. What she might say to *him* when the moment of departure came. Prior to the ugly scene in the Parisian shop, she had allowed herself to pretend that he might just tip her chin and look deep into her eyes and ask her if she would consider staying until spring...

But none of that happened. The train journey back from France was mainly silent and this time they drank no champagne. Cassie felt flat and empty as his car drove them back from the station and Giancarlo disappeared to his office the moment they arrived home.

Home.

Had she taken complete leave of her senses? This felt *nothing* like home. It was just a tall, city mansion inhabited by a man who saw what he wanted and ruthlessly went out and took it. Maybe it was because the woman he had loved had dumped him for his twin brother but—whatever the *reason*—he would never change. Why should he?

She booked her ticket back to Cornwall without telling him and when he arrived back from work she told him that she was catching the train first thing in the morning.

'That soon?'

Cassie hesitated. 'Well, yes. I...think it's best, don't you?'

He studied her face and, eventually, nodded. 'Maybe it is. But you don't have to travel by train, *bella*—my driver will take you.'

'It's very kind of you,' she said stiffly, 'but I'd prefer the train.'

'Why?'

Was he entirely lacking in comprehension? Couldn't he see it from her point of view? Of course he couldn't.

Giancarlo had been hurt and betrayed once in his life and, since that day, he had been building higher and higher barriers around his heart. He didn't let anyone inside them—and maybe they'd grown so high that he couldn't see the outside world with any degree of clarity.

'It's a small village,' she explained awkwardly. 'And people will gossip if I turn up in a big, chauffeur-driven limousine.'

With a stab of guilt, Giancarlo registered the whiteness of her face and the blue shadowing the delicate skin beneath her eyes. And in that moment he recognised that something had changed. He found himself regretting the bitter words they had spoken in Paris—but perhaps they had been inevitable. The smooth, sophisticated farewell he had wanted had been nothing but wishful thinking—because he had suspected for days now that she was reading more into the affair than he had ever intended.

But he would give her a night to remember. So that one day she would be able to look back and remember how good it had been. She would appreciate all that he had taught her—and her future husband would benefit from him having made her an exemplary lover.

'Okay, it is agreed—you will go by train. And now stop frowning, *mia bella*, and come upstairs with me. I want to make love to you—and I want it very badly.'

'But it's only seven.'

'I know it is.'

'And Gina will be preparing dinner.'

'I have given Gina the evening off.'

'Oh? And why would that be?'

'Because I want you on my own,' he growled.

Cassie felt pride warring with desire and desire won

hands down. Sliding her arms around his neck, she lifted her face to be kissed and silently forgave him. He hadn't broken any promises. Maybe she should commend him for that. He'd never filled her heart with false hopes—and if that heart was feeling wounded it was her fault for not having heeded his words. 'Then what are we waiting for?' she whispered.

The night which followed was bittersweet—the sex sublime—but Cassie found the hours between dawn and daybreak unbearably poignant as Giancarlo slept by her side and she stared wide-eyed at the moon-dappled ceiling. This is the last time I will lie here listening to his breathing, she thought, gently touching her fingertips to the rhythmical rise and fall of his powerful chest. Never again will I waken to the soft seduction of his kiss or to feel his limbs entwined with mine. Some day I may sleep with another man and make love with another man—but it won't be Giancarlo.

Next morning, she picked at a breakfast she didn't want and Giancarlo walked her to the door, kissing her one last time before putting her into the car with her single suitcase. She had told him to take all the clothes he'd bought her to the charity shop—and his face had darkened as he had demanded to know why. Falteringly she'd told him that there would be nowhere to wear them back in Trevone—and how on earth could she explain to her mother that she happened to have acquired a whole heap of designer clothes on a shop assistant's salary?

But just before he closed the car door, Giancarlo leaned inside and placed a turquoise box tied with a white ribbon into her hand. Cassie stared down at it.

'What's this?'

'It's a present.' His lips curved in gentle mockery.

'Don't you know that this is the time of year for giving?'

'But I haven't got anything for you.'

For a moment he hesitated as a mixture of guilt and desire heated his blood, thinking that she had given him the greatest gift a woman could give a man—her purity and her innocence. 'You've been the best present a man could ever want, *cara*,' he said softly. 'Just don't open yours until Christmas morning.'

The car pulled away from the kerb and automatically Cassie found her fingers closing tightly around the box—as if wanting to treasure it as the last thing he had touched. And it was only when they were safely away from the elegant crescent and the possibility of being seen that she allowed the tears to fall.

CHAPTER SEVEN

CASSIE couldn't wait until Christmas morning to open Giancarlo's present. The turquoise box burned a hole in her pocket all during the long train journey back to Cornwall—when the carriage was all noisy with revellers going home for the holidays.

Was it her imagination or did everyone seem happy and smiling and filled with hope and expectation? Was it only her who felt as if someone had squeezed her heart very tightly and left it all bruised and hurt?

She felt a fraud as she greeted her mother with a big hug—as if she'd changed beyond all recognition while she'd been away. And that the person who laughed and admired their ancient little silver Christmas tree was an imposter; the real Cassie far away in the remembered bliss of a cynic's embrace.

She tried her best to get into the festive spirit, the same way as she always did. She went to the pub on Christmas Eve. Gavin was there—along with a whole bunch of other people she knew. But again, she experienced that strange sensation of no longer feeling part of anything. As if Giancarlo had taken her away from her safe little harbour and cut her adrift—and she no longer knew where she belonged.

'Where's lover boy?' questioned Gavin. 'Not joining us tonight? Not flying in by helicopter for a quick pint?'

Cassie gave a smile which she hoped was less wan than it felt. 'No. It's over between us, Gavin. It was only ever a temporary thing. I told you that's how it was.'

'And you're okay with that?'

Behind her glued-on smile, Cassie gritted her teeth. '*Absolutely* okay with that.'

But later that night, when the midnight bells were chiming around the village and the ever-present roar of the waves from the nearby sea was sounding in her ears, Cassie knew she could wait no longer. Climbing into bed, she untied the white ribbon from the turquoise box and began to open it, her fingers flying to her lips as she looked inside.

For sitting on dark and luxurious velvet was a fine platinum chain from which hung a single bright diamond the size of a small pea. As she lifted it out it seemed to capture the light and sparkle it back at her in a rainbow cascade—and Cassie could have wept, knowing that she would never be able to wear it. At least, not in public. It wasn't the kind of jewellery you could pass off as fake since even the most untutored eye would have recognised its worth. So she wore it hidden beneath her dress on Christmas Day—and the cold stone which dangled against her skin felt like a constant reminder of the man who had given it to her.

And when she started back at work just after the New Year the shop seemed doll's-house tiny after the mega-stores of London. It was hard summoning up her customary enthusiasm—especially when Patsy, her boss, wanted to know all about working at Hudson's and Cassie wasn't mad-keen to relive any of it.

'Did you feel you learnt a lot there?' Patsy questioned. 'And in London generally?'

'Oh, masses,' said Cassie truthfully as guilt scorched through her. Imagine if Patsy knew the truth—that she had been accused of theft and sacked because a man with black eyes had made her concentration fly out of the window.

But the shame of losing her job paled into insignificance when measured against the pain of missing Giancarlo—a sharp, searing loss which seemed to haunt her every waking moment. All she could do was keep telling herself over and over again that she *would* get over it. It might take time but she would—because didn't they say that nobody ever died of a broken heart?

Throwing herself into work, she volunteered to redress the shop window and Patsy was flatteringly pleased with the results. Cassie suggested that they might have a preview evening for customers—offering wine and snacks—whenever the season's new stock came in and the idea was received with enthusiasm. She was promised a pay-rise in the spring and she tried to focus on the thought of the winter evenings growing lighter and the primroses pushing their pale yellow heads through the cold earth.

The only fly in the ointment was the slight queasiness she felt upon waking each morning. At first she thought it was because she'd been eating badly since getting back. Wolfing down squares of chocolate at inappropriate times, which she put down to Christmas greed—and showing a marked lack of interest in eating normal food, which she blamed on missing Giancarlo. It was easy to blot things out, when you really wanted to. And denial was easy, Cassie discovered—a safe and comfortable place to be.

Until one morning when she was actually sick— retching quietly in the small bathroom, terrified that her mother would hear and guess at the awful fear which was daily growing larger in Cassie's mind.

She waited until her mother had gone to her weekly salsa class before she dared do a test. Even buying the kit had seemed as if she was jinxing herself. She told herself that it was bound to be negative, that they'd used contraception every time—she told herself that because she refused to consider any alternative scenario. It *had* to be negative!

But it wasn't.

It wasn't.

It was glaringly and frighteningly positive.

Cassie went to bed, huddled beneath the duvet and pretended to be asleep when her mother got back. For the next five days she carried on trying to convince herself that there had been some awful mistake when deep down she knew there had not. And that she had to tell him.

In a way, the phone call was made worse by the realisation that Giancarlo *had* meant what he'd said. Because if there had been a small part of her which had longed for him to retract his words and go back on his intentions, then she had been sorely disappointed. There was no change of heart from her ex-lover. No emotional telephone call on Christmas Day, telling her how much he was missing her—even though she had stared at the phone and willed and willed it to ring. Nothing on New Year's Eve either—the other prime time when people allowed sentiment to take over from sense. He had meant what he said. It was over—and he had planned never to see her again.

Even making the telephone call required careful planning—it mustn't be anywhere where she could be overheard, and she couldn't make it outside because of the freezing weather and the ever-present pounding of the sea.

In the end she called when her mother had gone out for the day, praying that he would pick up and not let the call go through to voicemail. Because she couldn't tell him in a recorded message. She *couldn't*.

Pick up, she urged silently as she listened to the ringing tone.

Pick up!

'Cassandra?'

She was so startled by the sound of his richly accented voice that for a moment she was rendered speechless by a hundred different emotions, of which longing and sadness were the main ones. But she had never heard that note of wariness in his voice before—a note which told her more clearly than words that this was not a welcome call. If she had simply been calling on the off chance that he might want to see her again she would have ended the conversation as quickly and with as much dignity as possible. But she was not in a position to do such a thing. And how on earth did she even begin to tell him her momentous news?

'Giancarlo. I need to speak to you.'

At the other end of the phone, Giancarlo frowned, wondering what had made her abandon the pride he had so admired in order to ring him. Was she calling him on some flimsy pretext—the supposedly forgotten pair of earrings she had neglected to take with her, or the book she had been reading, which she had left behind? Was this a ploy to get back into his bed—and, if so, wasn't there a small part of him which was tempted to indulge her? For hadn't he missed the warmth of her beautiful body in his arms and the sight of her sweet smile greeting him when he returned from work each day?

'Giancarlo, are you still there?'

His eyes narrowed as he noted the lack of affection or everyday courtesy in her voice. This was not the wheedling tone of a woman who was prepared to trample on her own pride to get him back—and his senses were immediately alerted.

'You *are* speaking to me,' he pointed out coolly.

'I meant…in person.'

'In person might be difficult.' He thought of her firm young body. Her violet eyes and rose-petal lips. The way her hair had spilled like a pot of pale gold all over his bare chest. Yet what would be the use of seeing her again and letting temptation distort his thinking? Long-term she was an unsuitable consort for all kinds of reasons—he knew that and he thought that *she* had known it, too. This wasn't going anywhere—and maybe he needed to spell it out to her. 'I have a business trip coming up. Time is tight, Cassandra—you know how it is.'

In her little Cornish sitting room, Cassie flinched, wishing that she'd just come right out and told him—for then she would not have had to face the reality of hearing that note of cold dismissal in his voice. And hadn't there been a part of her which had hoped that maybe he was regretting letting her go? The little-girl part of every woman who clung onto a dream that he might want her back in his life—even when that was a hopeless and foolish fantasy? Well, she had just received her wake-up call because he very definitely didn't.

And, meanwhile, the harsh reality was that she still had to tell him…

'I'd prefer not to have to tell you this on the phone.'

'Tell me *what*?'

She swallowed. What else could she do but come right out with it? 'I'm pregnant, Giancarlo.'

The world tipped on its axis. Giancarlo heard the rapid thunder of his heart and felt a sensation of complete and utter powerlessness. And then anger. Pure and blinding anger.

'You can't be pregnant,' he said flatly.

'I can assure you that I am.'

His mind raced as he wondered how or when it could have happened when he had made sure that he had protected them—even though at times he had wanted her so badly that the short wait to don a condom had felt like an eternity.

'How pregnant?'

'Only a few weeks.'

He felt the heavy beat of foreboding while anger continued to pulse through his veins like all-pervading poison—so that the words came out before he could stop them. But didn't the cornered and powerless side of him want to lash out, and to hurt her? 'And you're quite sure it's mine?'

Cassie sank down onto the sofa as if he had struck her, temporarily winded by the harsh cruelty of his accusation. The blood pounded in her ears. Did he think that she was so hungry for sex and so easily able to forget him that she could have leapt from his arms, straight into the arms of another? And can you really blame him if he thinks that? Didn't you give him good reason to think that with the way you just fell straight into bed with him?

But in the midst of her hurt and her shame that he could think so little of her Cassie felt the first faint flicker of something she didn't recognise. Something primitive which had empowered women since the beginning of time. Suddenly, the stark and unwanted news became a miracle as her fingertips strayed towards her belly, fluttering like a butterfly as they drifted over the still-flat surface before coming to rest there protectively.

For a moment she just sat there as Giancarlo's words filtered back into her mind. Hateful, hurtful, unforgivable words in the circumstances. *You're quite sure it's mine?* How could he possibly ask her that when she had given him her virginity as well as her heart?

She sucked in a shuddering breath and the fingers on her belly curled into a determined little fist. 'No, *it's* not yours,' she said bitterly. 'The baby is mine—all mine! You don't have to do a damned thing—in fact, you can stay away from us, Giancarlo, because we don't want you or need you! I told you because I felt that it was your right to know—that's all.' And with that, she slammed the phone back down on its cradle and sank back against the cushions on the sofa.

Remembering that her mother would be back at some point, she forced herself to recover something of her equilibrium by realising that she was going to have to start looking after herself from now on. That she had a responsibility to the new life which was growing inside her. She needed to make plans—but she needed to do it without outside influence or pressure. No need for her mother to know. Not yet. Or Patsy. In fact, no one at all need know until she had decided how best she was going to cope.

There had been only one person in the equation who'd had any right to hear her momentous news and he had treated that announcement with contempt. For now, the most important thing was taking care of herself with good food and plenty of rest and working out what to do.

But she needed to get out of the house before her mother came back—took one look at her pale and tear-stained face and guessed at the huge change which had taken place in her life.

Wrapping up in warm layers and cramming a woollen beany over her plaited hair, she set off for a walk.

The ocean wasn't far away from anywhere in the village—that was one of the best things about it. Everywhere you went you could hear it swishing away in the background. There was something oddly comforting about its relentless motion and constant presence and Cassie wondered how many little human dramas it had lain witness to. How many women like her had walked along its shores while salt droplets had mingled with tears on their cold cheeks and they railed against men who didn't want them?

On a grey, January day like today the mood of the water reflected her own inner turmoil as giant breakers foamed up from the grey waters and crashed down onto the shiny dark slate rocks. All around her the wind howled like a caged beast and even the gulls sat motionless on the rocks—the gusts of air too violent for them to risk flying.

Cassie walked up the coastal path which led over the cliffs—a walk she had done countless times—and which usually left her feeling exhilarated and glad to be alive. But today her head was so full of troubled thoughts that it made counting her blessings a real challenge.

On and on she walked, until, aware of the fading light, she set back for home—still trying to work out some of the practical problems which lay ahead. At least the fresh air and exercise had left her feeling better and reinforced the fact that she was young and fit and could face anything. And at least she had a supportive mother and a roof over her head—women had brought babies into the world on much less than that.

But as she approached the final descent towards the village she narrowed her eyes in disbelief. For striding along the coastal path towards her was a figure which had once been so dear to her, but who now seemed to strike misery at her heart.

Giancarlo.

Giancarlo?

Clothed completely in black, he seemed like the personification of the devil. His black hair was windswept, his eyes were sending out ebony sparks—and the angry set of his features made him look positively forbidding.

She didn't call or say a word, even though the wind had now dropped, bestowing the atmosphere with a quiet, almost unworldly air. And it was only when she was close enough to see the hard glitter of his angry eyes and the set displeasure of his rugged features that she spoke—the words sounding as if she were reading them from an autocue.

'How did you get here so quickly?'

'I drove.'

'What, abandoned your oh-so-important meetings?' she questioned bitterly.

'My priorities seem to have shifted in the light of what you said on the phone.' Black eyes blazed. 'So what was it, Cassie—did you look at my lifestyle and my wealth and decide that you wanted some of it? Did you decide that a baby could guarantee you a lifetime meal ticket and catapult you into a different stratosphere altogether? Was that the reason behind your inexplicable refusal to let me buy you a coat in Paris? To lull me into a false sense of security before you made your coup de grâce?'

There was a moment of stunned and painful silence before she turned on him, her gloved hands clenched into fists by her sides. 'How dare you? I didn't *plot* for this to happen—it just did! Pregnancies do, Giancarlo—and, if you remember, *you* were the one who said you'd take care of contraception! And if you think I'd willingly choose a cold-hearted bastard like you to be the father of my child, then you are labouring under a big fat illusion!' Cassie swallowed, the excess of emotion making her feel dizzy. 'Anyway, you've made your feelings on the subject transparently clear—just as I thought I made mine. I told you that I didn't want you or need you—so would you mind telling me what you're doing here?'

Giancarlo looked into her pale features. Had he thought that somehow it wouldn't be true? That he would arrive and she would bite her lip and tell him it had all been a silly mistake and she'd misread the instructions on the test? But Giancarlo could tell instantly that there had been no mistake. Something about her had changed. Some new quality had entered those violet eyes and there was an unfamiliar detached expression on her face as she looked at him His mouth hardened. Did she think that he wanted this any more than she did?

But somewhere along the way—between the phone call and hearing her passionate defence—his own anger had fled. The situation had not been one of his choosing, but he would now mould it to suit his needs, the way he always did. His ability to be flexible had been one of the factors behind his incredible success—and Cassandra Summers would not stand in his way.

His eyes flicked over her assessingly. 'I have come to tell you that we will be married,' he said.

CHAPTER EIGHT

ACROSS the divide of the coastal path, Cassie stared at her black-eyed Italian lover as he came out with his extraordinary statement. For a moment, she wondered if the raw cawing sound of the circling seagulls had distorted what he'd said. But he had meant every word—she could tell that from the cold, grim look on his face, as if he had just been forced to do something against his will. And of course, he had, hadn't he?

Opening her mouth to answer him, she could hear nothing but the screaming birds and the helpless thunder of her heart. 'What...what on earth are you talking about, Giancarlo?'

'I am talking about marriage!' His mouth hardened as another blast of cold wind gusted through his hair. 'A marriage to legitimise the child we have created between us.'

It was a bald declaration and completely lacking in romance but, in a stupid way, Cassie was grateful for that. Because it meant that she could deal with it in an equally cold-blooded way—even though once she would have rejoiced at the thought of Giancarlo making such a proposition.

'But we no longer live in that kind of world!' she

protested. 'Where couples have to wed just because the woman's pregnant.'

His eyes were icy. 'You think that perhaps there is an alternative?'

'Of…of course there is. We can work something out—there are plenty of civilised ways of going about this. Women do it all the time.'

'Not with my child, they don't!' he snarled.

'Listen.' Cassie sucked in a deep breath, knowing that she needed to stay calm. 'I will never deny you access, Giancarlo—I promise you that.'

'You will never deny me access,' he repeated incredulously. 'Do you think you hold all the power, Cassandra?'

'But this isn't about *power*! It's not some boardroom battle which you've got to win!' she answered, thinking that pregnancy could make a woman strong. That the new life growing inside her could help her throw off some of the fears which had blighted her old life. And she would not let her rich lover trample all over her. *Ex*-lover, she reminded herself bitterly. 'It's about a *baby*!'

He sucked in a ragged breath as shadows of the past came back to haunt him. 'You think I don't know that? That I would be here if it weren't for a baby?'

Cassie flinched as he unwittingly told her how little she meant to him. 'No, I wouldn't dream of making so fundamental a mistake as that,' she said dully.

'Then what kind of man do you think I am? One who will walk away? Or one who can just be fobbed off—who will stand on the sidelines while you control the fate of my child?'

'And you think that *offering me marriage* will make

it better?' She thought about the reality of the situation. A marriage between a billionaire and a shop-girl—a woman he had chosen to have no more than a three-week affair with. Was he out of his mind? 'Tell me how that's supposed to work?'

'We will make it work,' he ground out. 'Because we have to. Because there is a baby and we owe it to that baby.' The thought of his seed growing inside her made his gut clench with unfamiliar emotion—but he could see the terrible whitening of her face and could not be sure whether the faint sway of her delicate frame was due to the bitingly cold air or to shock. And suddenly he was appalled at himself. That he should rail against a woman who was with child! Cupping her elbow with his hand, he was taken aback by how frail she felt beneath the waterproof jacket she wore and his face tensed. 'And we cannot talk here. Come. *Veni.*'

She was aware that he was guiding her down the path to the small car park, where his car sat beside the churning sea, looking incongruously luxurious with its black and gleaming bodywork. And never had she been more grateful for its cushioned warmth as she climbed in the back seat, with Giancarlo sliding in beside her.

He turned to her as she pulled off the woollen hat— thinking that the single plait of hair which tumbled down made her look ridiculously young. 'Who else knows about this?'

'No one.'

'Not even your mother?'

'Especially not my mother.' She met the question in his black eyes and gave a hollow laugh. 'Funnily enough, mothers aren't crazy about their daughters getting pregnant by men they've only just met and then split up with.'

'She knows the nature of our relationship?'

'Of course she doesn't! She knows I…met someone.' And hadn't Cassie seen concern pleat her mother's brow as she had gently tried to ask her daughter if anything was wrong?

'But she will approve of our marriage,' he said slowly. 'She will approve of me.'

It wasn't a question, Cassie realised—but a proud statement. And she supposed that when you were stunningly successful and powerful and had always had every woman you wanted—bar the one who had broken your heart—you would develop a certain arrogant pride in your own worth. To Giancarlo's mind he was exactly the kind of catch that every mother secretly wanted for her daughter. 'Because you're rich, you mean?'

'Because I will be able to provide for you, and our child.' His voice dipped. 'But approval—while preferable—is not essential. For I will never give up what is rightfully mine.'

Rightfully mine. His words of stark possession appalled her—even though she understood exactly where they were coming from. Cassie stared into the determined set of his proud features, remembering how his family inheritance had been taken by his twin brother because of an accident of birth. And because of that, a baby would mean more to him than to most men, she realised. This baby was going to be his first-born. The child who would inherit. The child he had never been. Suddenly, she saw just why he would never give up on his baby and a feeling of dread closed like a dark net over her heart.

'So it's a done deal,' she said, in a voice which sounded hollow.

'Indeed it is. I am glad that you are beginning to see sense, *mia bella*,' he said softly. 'All we need now is to work out the best way of presenting it.'

His thumb moved from his chin to his mouth in a slow, rhythmical movement as he caressed its cushioned outline reflectively. Cassie had seen him do this when she'd been living with him—usually when he was deep in thought and tussling over some business wrangle. But this wasn't about *business*, was it?

She stared at the narrowed eyes and the resolute light which gleamed from them. Maybe it was. 'And how do you propose we go about that, Giancarlo?'

His black eyes were brilliant as they met hers. 'We will marry immediately,' he said softly. 'But we will keep news of your pregnancy secret.'

'Why?'

'Because your mother is more likely to give her blessing if she feels that love is involved.'

'Oh, how...*cynical*,' she breathed.

'Or realistic?' he parried. 'People's lives and futures don't necessarily fit the story-book version, *cara*—and the world is less likely to be damning of the union if it is not sold as a forced marriage.'

Cassie felt sick. *Not sold*, he had said—as if he were in the middle of some wretched marketing exercise! And weren't his concerns more about his own pride and ego? Not wanting it to look as if he had been *forced* into marriage but had chosen it of his own free will. 'You're not exactly selling it to *me*,' she said in a low voice.

At this he stilled—and moved the thumb which had remained thoughtfully on his lips to rest on hers, and that contact made him start and take notice. How cold they felt in contrast to the warmth of his own flesh, he thought fleetingly. And wasn't he going about this in the wrong way? Wouldn't it suit his purpose to have her purring with pleasure—to use his considerable influence and sexual power over her to make her more accessible to his wishes?

'Aren't I?' he said softly, leaning towards her, his breath warming the icy tremble of her lips. 'How very remiss of me, *bella*. I wonder how best I can go about that? Mmm? Any ideas?'

His face was close. Too close. Close enough for its hard contours and aristocratic lines to mock her for what could never be. To make her long for the impossible. Cassie closed her eyes, knowing that he was going to kiss her—and, if she was being honest, she supposed that she *wanted* him to kiss her. To seal a deal which he had never wanted to make. But also because she had missed his kisses and all the closeness and intimacy which went with them.

He had tutored her in the sweet pleasures of the flesh and hadn't her newly awakened body ached for him? But at least by blotting out the sight of his mocking face she might be able to protect her emotions from the grim recognition that this was simply a business arrangement.

His mouth grazed over hers—and despite all the misgivings which stabbed at her heart it ignited instant fire in the pit of her belly. Back and forth his lips touched in light provocation, until the desire to put her arms around him overrode all other considerations like pride and self-respect. Biting back a small cry of something which felt like relief, Cassie clung to his shoulders as if she had found dry land after being lost at sea—and for a moment she felt safe as she let the kiss deepen and felt his tongue move inside her mouth.

He pulled her close, cushioning her silken hair in the palms of his hands and, after a while, he drew away from her, trying to steady the sudden shudder of his breathing.

'That is better. Much better. Now listen to me, Cassandra—for this is important. You will go home—and you will tell your mother that you are going to marry the man you met in London.'

Cassie swallowed. 'And if she asks me why?'

'You will tell her that you love me.'

'But I—'

'You don't love me?' he interjected mockingly. 'You know that and I know that—but that can be our little secret, Cassandra.'

'Another one?' she interjected bitterly. 'How many secrets will we have between us?'

He shrugged, still stroking her hair. 'In life, as in business—it is always wise to hold something back.'

'But this is different!'

'No, it is not different. The principle is exactly the same. Let's not overload your family and friends with too many surprises all at once.' His dark eyes glittered. 'And why don't we look at facts instead of fantasy? Love has never guaranteed matrimonial success—statistics show that arranged marriages fare much better.'

'N-not in the kind of world I've grown up in,' she answered shakily. 'And anyway, people are bound to be suspicious.

His mouth hardened. 'Then distract them by telling them that I am letting you choose a wedding venue any-where in the world. Give them something else to think about other than the speed with which the ceremony is taking place.'

For a moment, Cassie was torn between horror and admiration for the sheer cold-bloodedness of his proposal. He really *was* a cynic. Did he think that her mother would be swept away by the promise of a luxury wedding? Maybe he did. He had told her himself that he had a lifelong mistrust of women—and hadn't the only woman he had ever loved been blinded by the dazzle of wealth? The question was whether she should walk straight into an arranged marriage with such a man.

But what alternative did she have?

She tried to imagine the reality of going it alone as a single mother. Her mother's initial shock and disappointment would inevitably give way to affection—and any baby would be welcomed and adored into their little home. But it wasn't her mother's responsibility—and having a grandchild would impact heavily on *her* life. She was only just emerging from the grief of widowhood—and didn't she deserve a little freedom of her own?

Cassie thought about leaving a little baby while she went to work in the shop—and even if she got her promotion there would be hardly enough money to go round. She would be subjecting her child to a lifetime of making-do—while all the time the powerful and wealthy persona of his father would be hovering in the background.

And wouldn't Giancarlo be preparing to strike at the earliest opportunity? Eager to seize the chance to take the baby away from her. To whisk him or her off to London—or, worse, another capital city—where her child might become gradually inaccessible to her, protected by the impermeable barriers of great wealth.

There was something else, too—something she didn't want to acknowledge, even to herself. That the world seemed less frightening when Giancarlo was by her side. In a funny kind of way, he made her feel safe. He could make her heart leap with desire just by the brief brush of his lips. Somehow, he had the ability to make her feel alive—truly *alive*.

With a little nod of her head, she realised that capitulation was the only way forward—a sort of gritting her teeth and making the best of it.

'When?' she asked him. 'When shall I do this?'

'Do it today,' he commanded softly. 'And later, I will come and meet with your mother myself.'

So Cassie went home and broke the news that she was getting married. And she could see another reason for keeping her pregnancy secret. Deep down, wasn't she worried that her mother might try to talk her out of marrying Giancarlo—and wasn't it peculiar to discover that she didn't *want* to be talked out of it? As if by some wishful-thinking kind of magic she might be able to shuffle the hand that fate had dealt her and find something hopeful in the cards which lay before her.

In a slightly surreal state, she watched her mother's uncertainty become dawning delight when an impossibly elegant Giancarlo turned up on their tiny doorstep later that evening. The stern and serious expression on his face was tempered by the celebratory bottle of champagne he carried and, later, by the captivating quality of his smile.

Cassie felt appalled at just how utterly convincing and ruthless he could be in his pursuit of what he wanted. It was a side of him she had seen only once before—when he had bamboozled Hudson's into not charging her with theft. She listened as he vowed to her mother that he would look after her and said that they both wanted the wedding to take place as soon as possible—and that he hoped there were no objections to that. Maybe if it had been anyone else her mother might have had a few. But who in their right mind could object to Giancarlo when he was ladling on the charm with a trowel?

And it was only after he'd gone that her mother turned to her, a dreamy kind of smile on her face.

'Oh, darling,' she said. 'Now I can see *exactly* why you don't want to wait.'

Cassie managed a bright smile as she met her mother's eyes—her mother who had enjoyed a strong and loving marriage herself. What could she say? Because the truth of it was that part of her was longing to be Giancarlo's bride and to wear his ring on her finger—despite knowing how foolish her little dreams were. Was that what people meant when they talked about hope triumphing over experience?

They were married quietly, in London—because that had seemed the most appropriate venue after all. Giancarlo's offer of a wedding anywhere in the world had seemed like something someone else would do—not Cassie—and she was still smarting from all the accusations of being a gold-digger which he'd hurled at her. And so, despite only ever having been to Paris, she turned down New York and the West Indies and all the other luxury destinations he assured her were there for the taking.

She found herself caught up in a new and very efficient machine—one which was powered by money—and some of her new-found confidence seemed to desert her as a consequence. She would never have to save for anything again, she realised—with an odd little pang of nostalgia. Anything she and her baby wanted would be hers for the taking—and all she had to do was ask.

A hurried shopping trip produced a cream cashmere dress and jacket to protect her from the January chill—but the arum lilies which she carried seemed waxy and unreal. And, in contrast to the paleness of her own wedding outfit, Giancarlo seemed to represent everything that was black—with his jet hair and eyes and the dark, formal suit emphasising every honed fibre of his powerful body.

The wedding was small—Cassie's mother and Gavin were their witnesses and, although Giancarlo told her to invite anyone she wanted, she couldn't think of anyone apart from some of her school friends. And somehow it seemed *strange* to send out invites to a wedding when nobody knew them as a couple.

Because they weren't really a couple at all, were they? They were never intended to be—and if it weren't for his seed growing deep in her belly, then they wouldn't be here at all.

As the car drew up outside the registrar's office Cassie turned to Giancarlo—nervously fingering the white satin ribbon on her bridal bouquet. She looked up into the gleaming black eyes and longed for him to pull her into his arms, to tell her that it was all going to be fine. But the expression on his face seemed shuttered and tense, as if he couldn't wait for the whole day to be over. And hadn't she decided that she was going to be positive—to support him and be as much of a real wife as he would allow her to be?

'Didn't you want to invite any of *your* friends to the ceremony?' she asked him softly.

'No, I decided against it—it's all too much of a rush. Word might get out to the press and I'd prefer for that not to happen. Don't worry, *mia bella piccola*—you will be introduced to them all soon enough.'

Cassie stared down at her fancy cream wedding shoes, wondering if he was ashamed of her—or worried that one of them would try to talk him out of it.

'Now come along,' he urged softly as the bitter January air blew into the car, and Cassie shivered despite the warm cashmere. 'Time for you to become Signora Vellutini.'

The wedding band was a sliver of platinum which seemed too big for her frozen finger, and afterwards they ate lunch with her mother and Gavin at a discreet and slick hotel not far from Giancarlo's house. But despite the obstetrician she'd consulted in his plush Harley Street surgery assuring her that the occasional small glass of wine would be perfectly acceptable, Cassie could take only one sip of the fine champagne before quickly putting down the glass. It tasted sour. Acidic. Did her mother guess why she wasn't drinking alcohol? she wondered.

But it was clear to Cassie that her mum had a wonderful time—Giancarlo made sure of that. So much so that at times she felt almost like an outsider as she watched him employing more of that careless charm which had her mother laughing softly in response. *And wasn't that what had drawn her to him in the first place—that whole package of charisma and confidence and a determination to get what he wanted?* It just seemed like such a long time ago when he had strolled up to her little stand exuding danger and sex appeal and she had melted like candle wax. She felt as if she'd lived a whole lifetime since then.

Her mother left when the meal had ended—driven off in some style all the way back to Cornwall while Cassie and Giancarlo stood waving her off, her new husband's arm resting lightly around her shoulder.

'Your mother seemed happy enough,' he commented.

'Yes.'

He turned her in his arms to face him. 'You think she approves of your new husband, Cassandra?'

'You know she does.'

Giancarlo looked down at her, thinking how fragile and brittle she appeared—almost as if she might break in two. Like a china doll wearing her wedding finery. His eyes narrowed as he realised just how chalk-white her face was and the passion he had always felt for her was now tempered by a need to protect her, and to protect his baby. From now on, she must be cosseted, he realised grimly—for she did not appear to have been looking after herself.

'I think it's time to go home,' he said roughly. 'Don't you?'

Cassie touched the petal of a waxy lily and swallowed. 'Yes.'

But as the car drew to a smooth halt outside the massive town house she felt her stomach perform some kind of somersault. How peculiar it was to stand in front of that same house which had so intimidated her not very long ago. To now be able to call it *her* home. And to have the door opened by Gina—who surely felt much more comfortable in residence there than the new bride did?

The housekeeper smiled. 'Welcome home and congratulations, Signora Vellutini,' she said quietly.

Cassie nodded, feeling faintly ridiculous as she clutched her bouquet and gave Gina an uncertain smile. It was impossible to know what Gina was thinking—what was going on behind her own, rather formal smile. Did the housekeeper resent a new mistress coming into the house she had controlled for so long? she wondered.

'Thank you so much, Gina,' she answered quietly.

Once the housekeeper had gone, Cassie turned to Giancarlo and she reached out her hand to touch her fingers to the faint shadowing at his jaw. It seemed a long time since she had touched him—and she felt oddly nervous about doing so again. And maybe it was time to snap out of the strange, dreamlike atmosphere which had been present all day.

'Perhaps I put things a little clumsily earlier,' she said softly. 'I just wanted you to know that my mother had a wonderful time today, Giancarlo. Thank you.'

He moved her cool fingers from his face and kissed their tips, one by one. 'That is both my pleasure and my duty as your husband, *cara*.'

Husband. A little thrill of pride and possession ran through her as she stared up into his formidable features. She still felt disconnected from him—as if they had never been intimate as a couple before, and yet the growing life within her made mockery of that particular thought. Maybe that was what they needed. To become lovers again and to connect at the most fundamental level of all. Wouldn't that at least block out some of the harsh words they had spoken—and the realisation that he was only here under sufferance?

'Shall we—go to bed?' she asked tentatively.

Giancarlo looked at the dark shadows under her eyes and the lines of tension which had pleated her pale brow and at that moment he felt a twist of guilt. She looked so damned *young*. So impossibly *fragile*. He thought of the stress she had been under and the new life which was growing within her. Maybe that was why her face looked so strained that she resembled a sacrificial lamb more than a new bride.

'Bed is exactly what you need,' he said.

Cassie smiled as he took her upstairs to the master bedroom and stripped the clothes from her body as he had done many times before. But this time was different. This time there was no fire and urgency as he undressed her. His fingers were as light as feathers drifting over her skin. He seemed to be almost *restrained* as he carried her over to the bed and quickly pulled the silken cover over her—as if he wanted to shield her nakedness from his eyes. Was it possible that Giancarlo's desire for her had died?

And even as her body sank gratefully into the soft mattress she looked up at him in alarm—thinking how *distant* he seemed all of a sudden. Was he regretting that he had been forced to marry the mother of his child, or was he simply regretting not having invited his own family today, despite all the bad blood which had flowed between them?

Maybe he was thinking about Gabriella—the woman he *should* have married. And wishing that it were *her* who now lay naked and waiting in his bed. Was he? She had to know. She *had* to.

Some self-destructive urge took over and forced the question out—even though inwardly she prepared herself to be wounded by his answer. 'And what about your family?' she ventured as she looked up at him, wondering when he was going to get undressed and join her in bed.

Giancarlo stared down at the slender shape of her body outlined beneath the coverlet and felt an unmistakable kick of lust. 'What about them?'

'None of them there today.'

'I did not feel that it was…*appropriate*.'

'Do they…your brother and his wife…do they know about our marriage?'

'No,' he answered flatly.

Cassie sucked in a breath. 'But even if…even if things aren't good between you—don't you think you should tell them?'

He resented her intrusion—even though her words had hit home. 'I was planning to.'

'Oh? When were you going to do that?'

He traced his finger over one of the faint shadows beneath her violet eyes and registered the sudden tremble of her lips. She looked all in. And even though the soft curves of her body were screaming out for his caress, he forced himself to draw back from her—telling himself that he must temper his hunger until the roses were back in her cheeks. She needed rest, not passion—and at least he could provide that for her. His mouth hardened. And maybe bury a few ghosts at the same time.

'I thought I'd take you to Italy to meet them for yourself,' he said slowly. 'How does a honeymoon in Tuscany appeal to you, Cassandra?'

CHAPTER NINE

THE sleek black car moved through the darkening night and Cassie glanced out of the window, trying to quell her fluttering nerves. But it wasn't easy—not when Giancarlo sat beside her, as silent and as unapproachable as a statue as they headed towards his old family home.

Their honeymoon in Tuscany should have been the icing on the cake for a new bride who longed to know more about her husband's past and what had helped make him the man he was today. It gave her the opportunity to visit one of the most beautiful places on earth—and the chance to meet Giancarlo's twin brother, with whom he had fallen out so spectacularly, all those years ago.

But it didn't feel at all like that; it felt wrong—just as her life did. As if she was facing the unknown with a man who had become a stranger to her since their hurried marriage. And now she was heading towards a meeting which would intimidate the most confident of new brides.

The facts spun round and round in her mind. Giancarlo's twin was married to the woman who had shattered her new husband's heart and his trust in women. And not only was Cassie going to have to meet her and be judged by her—but she was also going to have to face up to something even more unpalatable. Something which seemed to make a mockery of their marriage and their future life together.

That Giancarlo had not made love to her since their marriage almost a week ago.

She had tried to make excuses for his blatant lack of interest—that he worked too hard and had too many high-powered deals going through at the moment. But that had always been the case, and it had never been like *this* between them. No matter what had been going on at work, he had always been hungry for her when he had taken her in his arms.

Yet now, he seemed to have acquired the knack of distancing himself from her—of seeming to be a million miles away even though they were alone together in the same room. The uninhibited lover she'd known during the days of their affair seemed to be a heady and distant memory.

On their wedding night, she'd fallen asleep before he'd come to bed and by the time she'd woken in the morning he was already up, behaving more like a doctor than a lover. Bringing her breakfast in bed and sternly making sure that she drank her herb tea and ate the plateful of scrambled eggs.

And afterwards, when she had tentatively tried to weave her arms around him, he had disengaged her and sternly told her that she needed to rest and recover.

Recover from *what*? she'd wondered as he had left her lying there—feeling slightly foolish—while he went downstairs to make the first of many phone calls.

The physical desert had continued during the next few days—and any brief contact from him had been solicitous rather than passionate. Without the reassurance of being desired, Cassie had felt her confidence trickle away. She felt as if he had tricked her—played some sort of cruel hoax on her by luring her into a marriage which had turned out to be empty. As if her pregnancy had made him stop desiring her—or perhaps he was just punishing her for having trapped him. *She was only with him because of the baby,* she reminded herself painfully. *And only a fool would forget that.*

They had flown by private jet to Rome and spent four days sightseeing before heading for the Vellutini estate—but when at last they drove through the grand gates of the Villa Serenita and she saw the enormous floodlit stone building ahead of her, Cassie could clamp down her questions no longer.

'How long is it since you've been here?'

He shrugged. 'Five years? Maybe six. I don't remember.'

'That's a long time.'

'Yes.'

Ignoring his monosyllabic response, she stared into the cold gleam of his ebony eyes. 'Is that because—?'

'It's because it's easier that way,' he said, with faint impatience. But Giancarlo's mouth hardened at her persistence and he wondered if she might ever take the hint. Hadn't he told her enough about the past? Hadn't she dug and dug to wheedle out more from him than he had ever intended her to know? About Raul. About Gabriella. And yet still she wanted more. Almost as if she wanted to suck him dry with her questions. 'That's just the way it's worked out. We meet up on or around my niece's birthday—usually in Rome, or Milan. It suits us all that way. It's no big deal.'

Cassie wasn't sure whether to believe him, but wise

enough to heed the cool note of caution which had entered his voice—and maybe it was crazy to quiz him just before meeting his twin. Even so, she couldn't help wondering if he felt envious when he looked at the massive Tuscan estate which could have been his. Or were his feelings still tied up with the woman who had chosen his brother? *The woman she was soon to meet.*

Rubbing a speck of dust off her brand new handbag, Cassie played safe. 'Tell me again—how old is your niece?'

'Allegra? She's twelve.'

'It's a pretty name. It's…strange to think of your brother being father to a girl who's nearly a teenager.' She shot him a shy glance. 'Especially when you'll soon have a tiny newborn.'

There was silence for a moment and Giancarlo felt the sudden lurch of his heart as he stared out into the Tuscan sky and the silver slither of the rising moon. A newborn. It sounded foreign. It *felt* foreign—because he still hadn't got used to the idea—and most times he blotted it out because it seemed almost beyond his comprehension. He had not intended to become a father and knew nothing about babies—and somehow it had been easier to pretend it wasn't happening. Safer too, since an online article he'd been reading had advised that early pregnancy was occasionally precarious and that babies could often be miscarried at this time.

And yet Cassandra's tentative words made the idea flare into reality in his mind. *A newborn.* Was it really possible—this miracle which had come on him so unexpectedly? His flesh and blood growing inside her even now? He recalled the photo which had illustrated the article he'd read—of a little blob with a big head and curled little limbs. Something which had looked unrecognisable and yet had unmistakably been the form of a baby.

Suddenly, he reached across and laid his hand over her still-flat belly, unprepared for her little gasp of surprise. 'Can you feel anything yet?'

She shook her head. 'Not yet. You can feel a flutter at about fourteen weeks, apparently. So there's still a little while to go.' She felt her cheeks begin to glow because she liked the sensation of his hand there. It made her feel safe and protected—and if you weren't loved, then surely those were pretty good substitutes. 'Are we...are we going to mention the baby?'

He looked into the darkened violet of her eyes. 'Not unless you want to make this even more difficult than it is.'

'You think it's going to be difficult?'

'No, Cassandra—I think we're all going to clasp hands and hug and laugh and joke together,' he said sarcastically.

Plucking at a soft fold of her cashmere coat, she wondered if he was about to smash all her stupid fantasies with one careless admission that she would only ever be second best. But she already knew that, didn't she?

Yet when she raised her face up to look at him she saw the unmistakable tension on his aristocratic features—and, despite her own feelings of worthlessness, she couldn't help her heart from twisting. Is he *hurting*? she wondered as he helped her from the car. Was this meeting going to be unbearably difficult for him—and could she do anything to help alleviate his pain? Well, she could try by biting back questions which made his emotions feel raw and concentrate instead on getting through the evening and making him proud of her.

'Just remind me,' she said softly. 'Your brother is Raul and your sister-in-law is called Gabriella—and Allegra doesn't have any brothers or sisters?'

'Sì, cara, esattamente,' he said softly, and paused. 'Ah, and here she is in all her glory to meet us.'

For a moment, Cassie thought he meant Allegra— because she remembered what she had been like at twelve. Could have easily imagined a young girl watching and waiting by the window, filled with excitement at the thought of seeing an uncle like Giancarlo. Yet it was not a coltish teenager who came towards the car, but a woman.

And what a woman.

Small and perfectly proportioned, her thick, glossy hair fell in a raven cascade over narrow shoulders. Her skin was olive, her restless eyes the colour of dark chocolate, and she wore an exquisitely cut dress in softest ivory—accessorised by brown crocodile-skin shoes. From her slender wrist dangled a narrow circlet of glittering diamonds and there were more diamonds at her ears—as well as a colossal solitaire beside her wedding band. On anyone else, that many diamonds might have looked showy—but the petite brunette exuded so much class and confidence that Cassie thought she could probably have worn a bin liner and convinced you it was haute couture.

So this, Cassie thought, was Gabriella.

Suddenly, she felt utterly insignificant in comparison—too pale and too wishy-washy with her fair skin and hair. Because this was the woman Giancarlo had *loved*, she reminded herself painfully. The woman he had *wanted* to marry—without anyone pointing a shotgun at him. The woman who had chosen his richer twin over him—and Cassie wondered whether a man like her new husband would ever recover from a blow so heavy to his pride and his heart.

'That's Gabriella?' she whispered.

'The very same.'

'She's…she's very beautiful.'

Giancarlo's mouth hardened into an odd kind of smile. 'Isn't she?'

Cassie felt her heart plummet. Her husband would have been a liar if he'd denied what was a glaring fact—but in that moment of terrible insecurity, what she wanted more than anything was for Giancarlo to tell her that the woman was a hag and he'd never loved her. But there was no time for further conversation, because the petite Italian beauty was upon them with a rush of heady scent and an unmistakable sparkle of her dark eyes as she stared up at her brother-in-law.

'Giancarlo,' she said, her hands moving familiarly to his shoulders as she offered him one cool cheek to kiss, followed by another. 'How good to see you again. It has been too long. Much, much too long. Nearly a year since we met you for dinner in New York!'

'That long?'

'I could tell you down to the very second,' she pouted. 'And in the meantime, you went and got married without even telling us!'

'But I thought you liked surprises,' he said archly. Stepping away from Gabriella's embrace and the overpowering scent of her perfume, he rested his hand lightly at Cassie's waist. 'And besides, I've brought my wife to meet you. This is Cassandra.'

'Your wife!' exclaimed Gabriella. 'Sometimes I thought I would never hear you say those two words! How happy I am to meet you, Cassandra.'

Cassie felt a bit like a trump card which had just been produced in a game of cards which had gone on for a long time with no sign of ending. She felt excluded by shared history and the dark undercurrents which flowed between the two of them—and found herself wishing that Giancarlo would do something significant and proprietary. Like planting a possessive kiss on her lips which would leave Gabriella in no doubt that he was completely enraptured by his new wife. But that wouldn't be true, would it? And perhaps she should be glad that he wasn't making empty gestures in order to gloat in front of his ex-lover.

'I'm very pleased to meet you,' she said politely, swallowing down her nerves. 'But please call me Cassie—it's only Giancarlo who uses my full name.'

'How *sweet*! Already you have nicknames for each other—because I gather this has all happened very quickly?' cooed Gabriella, hooking her arm through Cassie's as if they had been friends for years. 'So, I am dying to learn how you finally captured the heart of the man for whom all the women go crazy! You must tell me your secret, Cassandra—how you succeeded where so many others have failed.'

Was that remark supposed to remind Cassie about the only person who had *really* captured the heart of the Italian billionaire? Or to rub in the fact that she was not the kind of bride most people would have been expecting. A young and unsophisticated English shop-girl who felt all wrong, despite her expensive clothes—as if they were wearing *her* rather than the other way round.

'You'll have to ask Giancarlo about that,' Cassie answered as they passed through a stone arch into a courtyard and then into the vast house itself.

'Ah, but he is a man of mystery to me now,' sighed Gabriella. 'Who never tells me what is on his mind. Indeed, we rarely see him these days. A snatched moment here and there—that is all we must content ourselves with!'

'My brother is not here to greet me?' questioned Giancarlo.

'He has taken Allegra to look at a new horse—and the stables are miles away. He'll be back soon. But in the meantime, will you take some tea, Cassandra?'

'Yes, please,' said Cassie gratefully. 'I'd love some tea.'

'Then tea you shall have.' Gabriella slanted Giancarlo a smile. 'Do you want to come help me, *cara*?'

'As I recall, you used to employ a fleet of servants,' he observed softly. 'Which I'm sure you still do.'

'Ah, I see that your husband has lost nothing of his acid tongue!' Gabriella gave a graceful little shrug of her narrow shoulders. 'Very well, I'll go and organise it. But please do make yourselves at home.'

Cassie wondered if careless comments like that were what kept Giancarlo away. Home. A mocking reminder of what might have been.

She looked around. The room was beautiful in a faded kind of way and everything in it seemed very precious. Exquisite lamps spilled golden light onto the silken rugs which covered the flagged stone floors. There were sofas made from soft, dark velvet and gleaming wood which looked big enough to lose yourself in. Stunning Tuscan landscapes covered the walls and there was a portrait of a man whose proud, patrician features bore an unmistakable resemblance to Giancarlo.

Cassie walked up close and peered at it. 'Who's that?' she asked.

'My great-great-grandfather. He was a great singer and *bon viveur* as well as being the finest winemaker in the region. He was born here—as were his sons, and their sons.' He stared into black eyes so like his own. 'As was I.'

Cassie paused to let the significance of this sink in, hearing the unmistakable note of pride in his voice, and wondered if it hurt for him to have no part in this beautiful place. 'This house has been in your family for years?'

'Hundreds of years,' he agreed softly.

'Do you…do you feel regret when you look around and see what could have been yours?'

Giancarlo's mouth twisted into a sardonic smile. 'I'm over that, Cassandra. I'm not some deranged lunatic who counts all the family gold and secretly covets it. It's just a pity that my—*our* child will have no claim on its heritage, that's all.'

She heard his slip of the tongue. 'My' child, he had said, and that was what he had meant. She was simply the incubator. The vessel which carried the baby—not a woman he wanted as an equal. Not even a woman he even desired any more, it would seem.

But the sound of a door slamming and an excited shout woke Cassandra from her gloomy reverie and a young girl came running into the room, all long legs and long hair and muddy riding clothes—before hurling herself into the arms of Giancarlo.

'Zio Carlo! Zio Carlo!' she exclaimed, and then

said something in a stream of laughing Italian, until Giancarlo shushed her.

'In English, please,' he said sternly. 'For your new aunt speaks no Italian.'

The girl turned. 'Hello,' she said shyly.

'*Buona sera*, Allegra,' said Cassie.

'Ah, so my uncle is wrong—you *do* speak Italian!'

Cassie placed her thumb and her forefinger together to form a circle. '*Poco.*' She smiled. 'So he is nearly right!'

Allegra laughed and so did Giancarlo and for a moment Cassie felt a stupid thrill of pride—as if she had achieved the impossible by making him give that rare, low laugh.

'What's your name?' asked Allegra.

'Well, I was christened Cassandra—which is what your uncle calls me—though most people know me as Cassie.'

'It's a pretty name,' said the young girl shyly.

'Yes, it means "she who ensnares men",' came a voice from the doorway as Gabriella returned, carrying a tea-tray, an odd smile curving her coral lips. 'And that is exactly what has happened to your *zio*, Allegra—he has been ensnared at long last. Isn't that right, Giancarlo?'

Cassie felt her cheeks grow pink and wondered how he was going to bluff his way out of that one—but at that moment Giancarlo's brother appeared and the question was forgotten. At least, she assumed that it must be his brother—for the physical resemblance was strong enough to make her breath still in her throat, and yet... yet...

Surely this could not be Raul?

'Raul,' said Giancarlo. The action of rising to his

feet to greet his twin gave him a moment to recover his equilibrium—glad to be the owner of a face which gave away none of his feelings. But inside he felt the churning sensation of shock, which he quickly hid behind a bland smile.

Because his brother looked like a different man!

Tension was etched on his face and the black hair was touched with strands of silver. The features which were essentially the same as Giancarlo's own somehow seemed sharpened and there were deep lines etched into his face. Why, he looked almost a decade older than the last time he'd seen him—what the hell had happened to him?

'How are you, Giancarlo?' said Raul. 'Looking good, I must say. But then I hear congratulations are in order.'

His eyes swept over Cassie and for a moment they gleamed just long enough for her to realise that once this man must have been just as formidable and as gorgeous as his brother. What on earth had happened? she wondered dazedly.

'And this is your new wife?'

'Yes, I'm Cassie—and pleased to meet you,' she said politely.

'Really?' Raul's eyebrows shot up. 'Then I can only assume that for once my brother has been extraordinarily diplomatic—because he doesn't usually have a good word to say about me.'

'Ah, but that is because Giancarlo is floating on the pink cloud inhabited by the newly married!' said Gabriella brightly. 'Isn't that right, Carlo?'

Was it Cassie's paranoia, or did it sound almost as if Gabriella was *goading* Giancarlo to contradict her—to hear him denounce his marriage and his bride as necessities rather than choices? And suddenly she saw his determination to keep the pregnancy secret as good sense rather than cynicism. Imagine the field day that Gabriella would have had if she'd known that Giancarlo had been *forced* to marry her.

But it still begged the question why he had brought her here. All through dinner it nagged at her—creating a backdrop of disquiet while she struggled with the elaborate cuisine and took only a sip of the rich wine. At least she was sitting next to Allegra, who chattered brightly about England and her desire to visit it.

'Perhaps you could come to stay with us if your parents were agreeable?' Cassie asked tentatively, meeting Giancarlo's eyes with a question. 'Couldn't she?'

'Of course she could,' he said softly. For a moment he felt chastened by her instinctive generosity and the fact that she could make such an offer when the atmosphere over dinner had been, for the most part, as corrosive as he had dreaded it might be.

His sister-in-law had poured herself into a silk cocktail dress which was cut to cling to her petite form like a second skin. She had then proceeded to boast about her extravagant lifestyle in a way which had made him recoil—while she contradicted almost every remark Raul made. Even when his brother had been talking about his beloved art collection, Gabriella had been as negative as it was possible for a woman to be. He had noticed Cassandra biting her lip a couple of times and then deliberately engaging Allegra in a long talk about her horses—as if she was trying to dispel the poisonous atmosphere between the couple.

And maybe blood was truly thicker than water—for

the vestiges of Giancarlo's long-held anger finally dwindled away, to be replaced by a cold fury that Gabriella should treat his brother with such disrespect. And fury that *Raul was letting her*! Well, maybe it was time for his brother to listen to a few home truths.

Giancarlo waited until the end of the meal before rising to his feet. 'So, Raul—are you going to show me this art collection of which you are so proud?'

Raul shrugged. 'Sure, why not? Let's take a glass of grappa with us—and I'll give you a guided tour.'

Cassie watched them go, feeling suddenly isolated—especially when Gabriella turned to Allegra and told her that it was time for bed.

'But, *Mamma*—'

'It is late,' said Gabriella, her dark eyes glittering. 'Say goodnight to your aunt. And I will see you in the morning.'

Cassie hugged Allegra, thinking what a lovely girl she was and thinking how difficult it must be, living with two such obviously warring parents. 'And think about coming to stay with us in England,' she said.

'Oh, I will! I *will*! *Grazie*, Zia Cassandra.'

The two women sat listening to the sound of Allegra's footsteps clattering over the flagged stone floors on her way to bed—and once silence had descended Gabriella lifted one of the wine bottles and turned to Cassie.

'Drink?'

'Just water for me, thanks.'

Gabriella refilled her own glass. 'You're not much of a drinker are you, Cassandra?'

Cassie sipped at her water, determined that her pleasant smile shouldn't slip. 'Not really, no.'

'In fact, there's something I've been wanting to ask you all evening.' The Italian woman raised her perfectly plucked eyebrows in insolent query. 'Are you pregnant?'

CHAPTER TEN

CASSIE'S breath caught in her throat and her heart started rapidly accelerating as she stared at her sister-in-law, feeling as if she'd been caught out in some guilty secret. 'You dare to ask me whether I'm pregnant?' she whispered in disbelief. 'That's a very *personal* remark to make!'

'Which doesn't answer my question.'

'But I don't have to answer it. Anyway, lots of women don't drink alcohol,' said Cassie as Gabriella raised her glass to her lips.

'So they don't. But then, lots of women don't marry much older Italian billionaires either.'

'He's...' Cassie swallowed. 'Giancarlo's only fourteen years older than me!'

'*Only?* My dear—that's practically a different generation.'

'You know, I don't have to sit here and be insulted by you,' said Cassie quietly.

'I wasn't intending to insult you. I was just being honest with you—that's what family are for. Have you met any of his other friends? No? How come that doesn't surprise me? Well, I can assure you that I am only voicing what they will all be thinking. You see, you are not what I expected. Not at all. Giancarlo is an experienced and highly educated man of the world, while you... Well, I can understand that your gauche freshness might appeal to an older man's rather jaded palate—but when that fades, then what?'

Cassie's fingers tightened around her glass; she felt as if the blood were draining from her veins. 'Please,' she said weakly.

'I just think you should be aware of all the facts, Cassandra.' Gabriella's eyes glittered. 'You know that he was once in love with *me*? Wanted to marry me? Had his heart broken when I chose his brother instead?'

'Yes, he told me,' said Cassie woodenly.

'Oh, did he?' Gabriella drank another mouthful of wine. 'And the exquisite irony is that I made the wrong choice. Totally the wrong choice. For a long time now, I've been toying with the idea of ending the marriage— and giving Giancarlo the chance to pick up where he left off. What *do* you think he'd say if he knew that such an opportunity was here for the taking?'

Cassie didn't know what he'd say—all she did know was that if she didn't get away from there soon she would do something irrevocable. Like faint. Or hurl a glass of wine all over Gabriella's insulting face.

But through her anger and indignation that her hostess should have been so unforgivably rude came a terrible twisting of pain in her heart. Because what if Gabriella was speaking the truth? What if this was a terrible case of bad timing—with both Giancarlo and Gabriella having married the wrong people?

Raised voices heralded the return of the two men and Cassie lifted her head to look at them. Giancarlo's expression was a shuttered mask which gave nothing away—but she thought that Raul looked curiously at peace. As if some sort of weight had been lifted from his shoulders.

Giancarlo looked across the room at her and his eyes narrowed. 'Are you okay?'

From somewhere, Cassie summoned up a smile. 'Yes, fine—just a bit tired. I'd quite like to go back, if you don't mind.'

'Oh, stay!' said Gabriella brightly. 'There are plenty of beds.'

'Thanks for the offer, but we have a car waiting,' said Giancarlo, and turned to his brother. 'I meant what I said. Come and see me in London. Any time.'

'*Grazie*, Carlo.' Raul nodded. 'I will.'

Cassie was aware of the suspicion in Gabriella's eyes as they said their goodbyes and it wasn't until they were back in the car and headed out on the road to Rome that Giancarlo spoke.

'Well, that was an enlightening experience.'

Cassie hesitated, thinking how shadowed his face looked. 'In what way?'

He shook his head as he pulled a pulsating cell-phone from his pocket and began to read the screen. 'Just let me deal with this first.'

Cassie swallowed. Don't get irate. Don't tell him how rude he can be. It must have been a weird evening for him and she needed to be understanding. She waited until he had finished before clearing her throat. 'I thought Allegra was lovely.'

'She is. The one good thing to come out of that marriage.' Sliding the phone back into his pocket, he looked at her thoughtfully. 'Did Gabriella treat you properly?'

'She...well, actually, she guessed I was pregnant.'

He glanced down at her belly. 'That's not something we're going to be able to keep secret for much longer. But apart from that?'

She wondered whether to burden him with a word-for-word transcript of Gabriella's bitchiness but some instinct stopped her. *Because what if everything her sister-in-law had said was true?* Suppose she *was* holding Giancarlo back from what he had always really wanted? Wouldn't that force the subject out into the open? And then what? Questions like that required answers she might not want to hear.

'She was okay,' she said, with a shrug. 'Not really a woman's woman, I guess. But what about Raul? He... well, he looked much older than I expected. I could hardly believe he was the same age as you. Was everything all right with him?'

Was everything all right with Raul? Giancarlo's mouth tightened with irony as he recalled the demons which had flown from his twin brother's lips during their talk in the library, and he shook his head.

'No, things are anything but all right with Raul,' he said slowly, turning his head a little to watch the dark Tuscan landscape speeding by. From here he could see the indistinct outline of the countryside where he'd played as a boy. Played with his twin brother before ambition and money and a woman had driven a wedge between them.

'The marriage is on the rocks,' he continued. 'It has been for some time, apparently. I told him it was clearly damaging to Allegra as well as to each other—and if it can't be made better, then he should get out of it.'

'Oh. Oh, I see.' So he knew anyway. Raul had told him. A terrible fear began to prickle at Cassie's skin. Did

Giancarlo see what Gabriella saw—an opportunity for him to step in and take what should have always been his? And was he, like his sister-in-law, kicking himself because the timing was all wrong? That he had married his pregnant mistress at precisely the wrong moment. 'That's a pity.'

'Yes.' But he heard the odd catch in her voice and he looked at her more closely. 'You're trembling, Cassandra,' he said softly. 'Are you cold?'

Couldn't he see how his words now hung like the sword of Damocles over her head? She was nothing like Gabriella—and yet Gabriella had been the woman that he'd loved. Had he looked at the two of them to-night and compared them? One so sleek and dark and sophisticated—and the other a young, pale foreigner who could never compete, not on any level. 'A…little.'

'Then let's get you back.' Leaning forward, he rapped sharply at the glass partition which separated them from the driver. *'Piu velocemente!'* he ordered, his voice suddenly urgent.

The car drew up as close as it could get to their hotel, and they walked a little way in the crisp night air, back to their penthouse suite which overlooked the city's famous Spanish Steps. In the mirrored confines of the elevator Cassie could see Giancarlo's gaze raking over her assessingly and she wondered if he was thinking about the beautiful brunette they had just left. But then he placed his arm about her shoulder and drew her close to his powerful frame.

'Tired?' he questioned.

She shook her head. Her head was spinning from all that she'd seen and heard during dinner and the thought of sleep seemed impossible. 'No. Actually, I'm wide awake.'

'Me, too.' He thought how clear her skin looked and how bright her violet eyes. He thought of the pain and the bitterness on his twin brother's face as he had poured his heart out—and suddenly he wanted to blot it all out with Cassandra's sweet kiss.

'You know, you are really very beautiful,' he said softly. *'Sei molto bella,'* he repeated in Italian and began to kiss her—her stifled little cry of surprise sounding on his lips. For a split second she seemed to hesitate—as if the chemistry which had once burned between them were no more. And then she melted against him, opened her mouth beneath his as naturally as breathing and gave a little moan. He slid his arms around her waist and then brought her even closer, revelling in the sensation of her soft curves and the silken spill of her hair. How long had it been? he wondered hungrily—as his body gave a sudden urgent jerk of desire. Not since the night before she'd left London at Christmas...

'Giancarlo—' she said breathlessly.

'I want to make love to you, *bella*. I want to make love to you so badly.'

Why now? she wondered desperately. Why *now*? She opened her mouth to ask him but once again his powerful kiss silenced her.

Flagrantly, he rubbed his arousal against her belly—leaving her in no doubt about how much he wanted her. The loud ping of the elevator did nothing but temporarily interrupt his deepening passion as, with a low growl, he led her into their suite. Kicking shut the door behind them, he pushed her coat impatiently from her shoulders, let it slither to the floor before lifting her up in his arms and carrying her along the corridor towards the vast master bedroom.

'Put me down,' she protested. 'I'm too heavy.'

'You're as light as a feather,' he contested as he lay her down on the bed. 'Despite the fact that you carry my child inside you.' But the reminder of that made his fingers halt in the trembling process of unbuttoning her dress—despite the desire which burned inside him. He thought of the tiny life inside her and he swallowed down the hot cocktail of lust which was heating his blood. 'In fact, maybe this is not such a good idea after all,' he said unsteadily. 'I don't want to hurt you.'

Ironically, his momentary wavering killed her own uncertainty and she shook her head, her fingers clamping around his stilled hand. 'You won't. There's nothing in the rule-book which says that pregnant women can't have sex,' she whispered, moving him back in the direction of her aching nipples and closing her eyes with pleasure as he began to touch them.

'Isn't there?' he questioned unevenly. He bared her creamy breasts—fuller than he remembered them, and showcased perfectly in a filmy lace brassiere. Unsteadily, his fingers trailed over the outline of a tight, rosy nub and felt it pucker up beneath them, like a crushed petal. 'Are you sure about that?'

'Qu-quite sure.'

He peeled away her dress and slid off her stockings, bra and panties and then took off his own clothes—for he did not trust himself to wait while her trembling fingers tried to accomplish the task. And then, pulling her into his arms at long last, he groaned as their naked bodies made contact. She was all soft and giving flesh and he ran his fingers keenly over her skin, feeling the urgent jerk of his body in response.

'You feel amazing.'

'So do you.'

'It's been too long since I have felt your exquisite body in my arms,' he asserted hungrily. 'And I had forgotten just how good you feel.' Momentarily, he let his hand linger on the still-flat plane of her stomach before letting it drift down over the curving swell of her hips. And then down still further, so that she moaned softly into his ear as his fingers skated over the silk of her inner thigh.

'Our first time as man and wife,' she whispered. Yet momentarily the thought of that disturbed her, even as his hands began to work their magic—his fingers sliding between her thighs and finding her honeyed heat. Helplessly, she bucked beneath their questing touch, her lips brushing against his neck. She wanted to ask him why he had not touched her before tonight and what had provoked this sudden storm of passion. 'Giancarlo.'

'It's good?'

'It's…' But her question remained unasked. There was no need for words—nor any time for them—for Giancarlo was parting her thighs with the urgency of a man who could wait no longer. And she didn't want him to wait—she wanted him to heal her frayed nerves with the power of his body.

It was easy to urge him on with the helpless thrust of her hips—the silent plea for him to take her. Wordlessly, he interpreted her invitation and accepted it, entering her with one masterly stroke, and she gasped out loud as he filled her with his hard, hot heat. 'Oh, Giancarlo!' she cried. 'It's…'

'It's what, *cara*?'

It was pleasure so perfect that it dissolved all her fears as he moved inside her. It felt like a discovery—or a rediscovery—as if she had forgotten just how incredible it could be with each slow, high thrust. Wrapping her legs around his warm back, she tipped her head back to give him greater access to her eager flesh. His tongue rasped greedily over each breast and, with trembling fingers, she could feel the powerful tension in his buttocks as he spurred her on.

She thought that he had never been quite so passionate with her before—as if he could barely contain himself, saying things to her in fervent and breathless Italian. What did those words mean? she wondered fleetingly. But then it was too late to wonder anything—for the waves began with a sweet inevitability as her body began to shudder helplessly around him.

For a moment he stilled and just watched her—saw the uninhibited arching of her back and heard the little gasps which were torn from between her parted lips. And as the first flowering flush began to appear above her breast he drove into her once more—felt the heated welcome of her still-quivering body.

His own orgasm came upon him with unexpected intensity—it seemed to empty him of more than just his seed. And afterwards, he cradled her in his arms—felt the sheen of sweat on her soft skin and his finger found the pulse which skittered so frenetically at her temple. Her heart was beating so fast—and suddenly reality hit him with a cold fist.

Protectively, his hand splayed over her belly. 'I haven't hurt you?'

With a sinking heart, Cassie heard the concern in his voice as she realised that his bedside manner was back again—and the insecurities which making love had suppressed came flooding back with a vengeance. Had he hurt her? Yes, many times—but never physically. The powerful thrusting of his body did not bring the pain that his emotional distance did.

Through the muted light of the room, she stared into the dark gleam of his eyes. Was it simply coincidence that he had chosen tonight to make love to her for the first time since their wedding? And why had he spoken to her in that unaccustomed Italian in the middle of it all?

Was he imagining that it was Gabriella in his arms? Gabriella he was thrusting into? Was that what had inspired such a show of passion tonight of all nights—when he hadn't touched her since they'd said their goodbyes before Christmas?

Drawing in a deep breath, she looked at the shadowed perfection of his face, forcing herself to ask the question—because weren't married couples supposed to be able to communicate with each other? 'Do you ever wonder what your life would have been like if you'd married Gabriella?'

The subject of his sister-in-law shattered his warm contentment like a bucket of ice-water and, silently, Giancarlo cursed his wife for bringing it up. For a moment he didn't answer, even though a thousand responses leapt to his tongue. But he could see from the sudden trembling of her lips that she was determined to have an answer. 'But what would be the point of that?' he said slowly. 'Conjecture is a pointless exercise, Cassandra—I learnt that a long time ago.'

Cassie's gaze didn't waver. Was that about the same time he learned never to trust women? 'You should have been a politician,' she said lightly, even though her heart was thudding painfully in her chest. 'I've never heard such an evasive answer.'

'Is that a criticism?'

'Just an observation.'

His face darkened. 'And why the hell are you bringing up a subject like that at a time like this?'

Because she needed to know—and how could she possibly know if he never told her anything, if he kept everything so buttoned-up and close to his chest? She thought of Gabriella's bitterness about marrying the wrong man—which could have been provoked by regret and jealousy. But her sister-in-law had said something else, too…something which had also hurt. Something which could easily be proved.

Have you met any of his other friends? No? Well, I can assure you that I am only voicing what they will all be thinking.

Was Gabriella right? Hadn't Giancarlo deliberately kept her away from his friends before the wedding—and then neglected to ask a single one to the ceremony itself? As his mistress she hadn't been good enough to meet them—and it seemed that even as his wife she did not qualify either. Maybe he didn't intend for her to get to know them at all. Perhaps that was to be the way of it—with her increasingly being marginalised. The unsuitable bride who needed to be kept away from his powerful peers.

'You know, I still haven't met any of your friends, Giancarlo.'

'And?'

Fractionally, Cassie moved away from the distraction of his naked body and the warmth of his embrace, which did not match the sudden cold gleam in his black eyes. She drew a deep breath. 'And I'd like us to throw a dinner party when we get back to London.'

His eyes narrowed and then he shrugged before moving away from her. 'So do it.'

But just before he turned over—as if to halt any further conversation on the subject—Cassie saw the unmistakable tautening of his face.

CHAPTER ELEVEN

THE small blonde whirlwind which was his wife flew at him as soon as he had let himself in and Giancarlo stared down into her flushed face and listened to the words which were tumbling over themselves in their hurry to be heard. Lifting his hand as if he were quelling dissent at a board meeting, he shook his head. 'Enough.'

'But—"

'I said *enough*, Cassandra,' he reiterated softly. 'Because I don't give a *damn* if the trifle won't set! And neither am I interested in the consistency of the gravy. That's why I employ a housekeeper! Why the hell won't you let Gina do it all—the way she always does?'

Cassie bit her wobbling lip. Why couldn't he *understand*? Didn't he realise that sometimes she felt useless—like some little child who needed to have everything done for her? 'Because…because I want to do some of it myself—otherwise how can we possibly say that it's *our* dinner party?'

Giancarlo looked at her anxious face with mounting frustration. He'd agreed to a dinner party so that she could meet some of his friends—yes. What had not been part of the deal had been a near-hysterical pregnant wife who was taking on an unnecessary amount of work and appeared to be failing spectacularly to complete any of it. Picking things up and then putting them down somewhere completely different. Changing her mind and then changing it back again.

But then, she'd been positively mercurial ever since they'd returned from their honeymoon—her moods varying wildly from sweet to tearful with a hundred variations in between. His online pregnancy guide had informed him that women were victims of their hormones during this trimester—and that he must be patient. Patience wasn't an attribute with which he was particularly familiar, but he was trying. He had even drawn a veil over her prying persistence and the intrusive questions she had flung at him in Rome. His mouth hardened. Once things had calmed down she was going to have to learn he simply would not tolerate her raking up the past. But in the meantime he would humour her.

He studied her frozen little figure, his hands reaching out to massage away some of the tension in her shoulders. 'Listen to me, Cassandra—I've told you a hundred times that you don't have to *prove* yourself.'

'But, I do! They're *your* friends and they don't know anything about me—and I want...I want to make a good impression.' Shaking herself free, Cassie walked over to one of the vases which stood on the hall table and gave a piece of foliage an unnecessary tug. She had been gearing up to this dinner for days now and sometimes it felt as if she were taking an exam in social etiquette as she prepared to meet some of her husband's buddies. Hadn't she been reading all the broadsheet newspapers for days in preparation—stuffing her head with facts so they wouldn't think she was just some vacuous shop assistant?

Yet deep down she knew that much of her behaviour was because she wanted to prove to herself that Gabriella was wrong. That Giancarlo's friends wouldn't all be wondering why he had married her. That even when they found out about the pregnancy—which might very well be tonight, judging by her oddly distended stomach—they would still like her and think her the sort of person who was worthy of him. She turned away from the vase to face him. 'The meal will probably be a complete disaster,' she moaned.

'Just calm down,' he soothed. 'They're not coming to judge you.'

But that was where he was wrong. Of *course* they would be judging her—it was human nature to judge, especially when a shop-girl married a much older man who happened to be a billionaire.

She dressed for dinner and re-jigged the place-cards—frighteningly aware that the guests had travelled a long way for this dinner. Gianpiero and Serafina were Paris-based, and Nick and Kate were visiting from New York. Only six of them—because she'd felt that eight might be a bit over-ambitious—and now she worried whether six might make the big table look awfully *empty*.

Cassie had organised the menu, knowing that Gina disapproved of most of it, but telling herself that she didn't care. Because this was about more than introducing herself to Giancarlo's friends as his wife—it was about trying to define her role *as* his wife. It meant gently showing Gina that she wanted to be involved in the running of the house and that she wasn't just some docile little puppet of a woman.

But that was what she felt like. Sometimes she might almost have been invisible. It was as if she didn't count—as if she had no real place in a house paid for by her wealthy husband and run by his efficient house-keeper and his other members of staff. And wasn't this dinner also supposed to make Giancarlo see her as a *partner*, rather than an appendage? Not just some fertile little blonde quietly growing her baby in the background while he carried on working with the same intensity and dedication as he'd done as a broke young lawyer who'd first arrived in London.

This was supposed to be their first outing as a *couple*. Because even though their sex life had resumed since that night in Rome she still felt no closer to him. Wasn't this just another hurdle she had to leap over—to prove to him that she was someone he could trust? Someone he could confide in.

Fortunately, the simple dark dress she wore gave no hint of her burgeoning belly and she left her hair free to tumble over her shoulders. She'd chosen white hyacinths and tiny white narcissi with which to decorate the rooms and the whole house smelt heavenly.

And when Giancarlo emerged from his dressing room, looking formidable and yet heartbreakingly beautiful in a dark, dark suit which hugged the powerful body and drew attention to his muscular physique, she prayed that she would not let him down.

'Stop worrying,' he said as he saw the small frown furrowing her brow. 'They won't bite.'

Maybe they wouldn't—but Cassie still felt terribly intimidated when the two couples arrived. Kate was a sleek New-Yorker with a freckle-spattered nose, a lazy smile—and the most immaculate clothes Cassie had ever seen. Her husband, Nick, was 'something in films'—his suit was linen and slightly crumpled, but he exuded the indefinable air of the truly powerful. As for Serafina—she left Cassie wondering if there was such a thing as a plain Italian woman, and her banker husband was equally good-looking.

While having pre-dinner drinks in the drawing room, Cassie was so nervous that she slopped champagne over Kate's silk jacket.

'Oh, gosh. Oh, no. Oh, I am so *sorry*!'

'It doesn't matter. Honestly.'

'It only cost nine hundred bucks, didn't it, honey?' joked her husband.

'Sit down, Cassie,' said Giancarlo gently. 'And let Gina serve the drinks.'

She felt like a child who had been reprimanded—but maybe that wasn't so far from the truth. In many ways her life experience was as insignificant as a child's when compared to theirs. She didn't even get a chance to talk about the articles she'd read in the papers—or the news bulletins she'd tried hard to memorise. This rarefied group were all ten to fifteen years older than her and they seemed to want to talk about things she'd never heard of. Or people she'd never met and probably never would. Giancarlo's age had never seemed a barrier— but now, with this laughing glossy posse of friends, he seemed to have stepped even further beyond her reach. Maybe Gabriella had been right after all.

Her decision to serve a traditional English roast dinner was as ill advised as Gina had hinted. Cassie saw the slight narrowing of Giancarlo's eyes as a dish of mis-shapen Yorkshire puddings made their appearance—and she distinctly overheard Serafina asking Gina whether she still made her delicious home-made pasta.

'But I thought we'd try something different for a change!' said Cassie brightly.

Four pairs of curious eyes were trained on her.

'So where did you two meet?' questioned Gianpiero as he politely ladled a couple of sprouts from the dish.

'I was...I was working in a store, actually.'

A brief silence was filled in by Serafina. 'Oh! Which store?'

'Hudson's.'

'Hudson's? Honey, isn't that where you picked up that suit?' asked Nick.

Kate smiled back. 'It is indeed. Why, you might even have served me, Cassandra.'

'I doubt it. You see, I worked in the candle section,' said Cassie doggedly, just wishing that the floor would open her up and swallow her.

'Don't tell me Giancarlo was buying *candles*?' drawled Nick.

'No, I was much more interested in the person selling them,' he murmured, and they all laughed.

But the revelation about just how lowly her job had been made Cassie sink even further inside herself and the rest of the evening passed by in an embarrassing blur. The food tasted like stodgy sawdust and was only saved by some brilliantly strong Italian coffee and the expensive dark chocolate bought by Serafina. By the time the guests had left in a flurry of goodbyes and air kisses—she felt completely drained—as if all the life and energy had been sucked from her.

Giancarlo bolted the front door and looked at her as she slumped tiredly against the wall. 'So what was all that about?' he questioned softly.

'Which bit are you referring to?' she snapped. 'The

complete flop of the meal or the fact that I sloshed wine all over a thousand-dollar suit?'

'I'm talking about the way you sat there looking as if you were a witness at your own execution!'

'Can you blame me? Your friends don't like me.'

'That's complete rubbish. You didn't really give them a chance, did you?'

'Everything they said went way over my head. You were all talking about things I'd never heard of!'

'But that's hardly surprising—I haven't seen them for ages and I've known them for *years*—'

'While you've only known me for five minutes?'

'That's not what I meant,' he said frustratedly.

'No?' Suddenly, an odd feeling of weakness washed over her—as if she'd been battling and battling against some immovable force and had finally run out of strength. She shook her head. 'Look, maybe this is all a waste of time and we should just stop pretending to each other,' she said wearily. 'Maybe I should just give you your freedom—at least that way you can get together with Gabriella and have *some* chance of happiness.'

Giancarlo stilled. 'So that I can *what*? What did you just say?'

Cassandra shrugged. 'She's going to split from your brother—you told me that and so did she. She also told me that all of your friends were wondering why the hell you married me—and tonight proved her right. She still wants you—she made that perfectly clear. And I know you still want her, Giancarlo.'

There was a heartbeat of silence. 'And just how do you know that?' he questioned dangerously.

But Cassie was too distraught to heed the icy warning

in his voice and much too emotional to be able to bite back the words she had been bottling up for days now.

'Because you didn't lay a finger on me after the wedding, did you? Not until the day we saw *her*. Then you couldn't get enough of me—it was like you were wild for me that night.' The bitterness welled up, like an all-consuming cloud. 'Did you close your eyes and imagine it was her, Giancarlo?' she whispered. 'Her you were making love to—not me? Is that why you said all those things to me in Italian—things I couldn't even understand?'

There was a fraught and disbelieving silence. 'You think that?' His face had drained of all colour. 'You really think I am capable of such behaviour as that?'

Her mind was spinning so much that she wasn't sure what she was thinking any more and the thready beat of her heart was making her feel dizzy. 'It's the kind of assumption any woman might make under the circumstances.'

His stony words matched the sudden hard gleam of his eyes. 'Not if she had any respect for her husband,' he snapped. 'Or any respect for herself!'

At this, something inside her snapped back. 'How can I respect myself when I get nothing back from you? You never tell me what's on your mind. You never open up to me. I don't really *matter* to you, do I, Giancarlo—not as person? I never have, not really. I'm just a commodity—first a mistress and now a prospective mother. You don't want *me*—only what I can give you!'

He felt a slow kind of anger begin to burn inside him. How dared she confront him with this messy emotional display and outrageous allegations? 'Do you imagine that this kind of hysteria is going to win you any brownie points?' he flared. 'Don't you think that sitting down and having an adult conversation about what is troubling you might be preferable to throwing out a series of accusations when you're overwrought?'

She stared at him—and never had he looked more forbidding. Not even that windswept day in Cornwall when his rage had been dark and he had discovered she was pregnant.

But that had been when she'd decided to go it alone—when her pride had been intact, not slowly being dismantled by her unrealistic yearning that one day he would learn to love her. Because he would never do that. She should have stuck to her guns and kept her integrity and been that single mother who could hold her head high. Who wouldn't keep pushing and pushing for a little love and affection and coming up against an emotional brick wall, time after time. But maybe she could still do it. Maybe it wasn't too late to claw back a little independence.

'You…you… You cold-hearted *machine* of a man— you'll never understand! You wouldn't be able to interpret the facts if they jumped out and punched you! Well, I'm through with trying to pussy-foot my way round your brooding silences and attempts to stonewall my conversation. Having to bite back questions all the time because Mr Moody doesn't want to answer them!'

Cramming her fingers in her mouth to stifle her sobs, Cassie rushed straight past him, running upstairs to the spare room where she locked the door and stumbled into the bathroom to let the tears begin to slide from her eyes.

She cried until there were no tears left—until her body and eyes felt dry and sore and aching. Her head felt tight and so did her stomach as she crept from the bathroom and lay on the bed and wondered what on earth she was going to do next.

Should she tell Giancarlo that, despite their bitter and angry words, maybe it was best that it was all out in the open? That they couldn't carry on ignoring the fact that the marriage wasn't working—and that a baby certainly wasn't going to make it any better. If he knocked on her door and demanded to be let in, she would open it and they would calmly talk it all out until they had worked out some kind of way forward which would be satisfactory to both of them.

But he didn't knock—and in a way that shouldn't have surprised her, for Giancarlo was not the kind of man to meekly turn the handle of a locked door and ask to be let inside. She would just have to wait until the morning, when they could discuss things in the cold light of day. And she would have to face the future with a heart which felt as if it were breaking in two.

Kicking off her shoes and still wearing her dress and stockings, she crawled beneath the coverlet and lay there, shivering and drifting in and out of sleep.

She didn't know how long had passed when her eyes snapped open in alarm, her senses alerted by some dark instinct—knowing that something was wrong.

Terribly wrong.

She just didn't have a clue what it could be.

She felt a sharp spear of pain low down in her abdomen—accompanied by the frightened jerk of her body. For a moment she just lay there—too scared to move— until tremblingly, she slid her fingers down between her thighs and their tips came warm and sticky. And she didn't need to snap on the bedside lamp to see that they were covered in blood.

An intense shudder of shock and fear ran through her—the kind of fear she had never known before. She opened her mouth to call out—but no words came. Sucking in a deep breath, she tried again—calling out the only word she could think of in the mists of this pain and fear.

'Giancarlo!' she screamed. 'Giancarlo!'

CHAPTER TWELVE

GIANCARLO hadn't been asleep. He had been lying there fully dressed—staring blankly at the ceiling, wondering, with a curiously heavy heart, just why he was in one great big bed, while Cassandra was a few yards away in another.

Because she was a stubborn and wilful woman, that was why, he thought grimly. Too stubborn to understand the subtle complexities of life. *His* life. Couldn't she see that he had a history and a way of living which were already established—and that it was her place to slot right into them? Yet she couldn't have made it more difficult if she'd tried.

Did she think that by going off to sulk in the spare room she would be able to manipulate him to *her* will and way of thinking? Did she really think he would allow her to trample all over his feelings? Well, she was about to learn a very stark and hard lesson.

And then he heard it. A terrible, blood-curdling scream which clutched at his heart with an emotion which was pretty much unknown to Giancarlo.

Fear.

He leapt out of bed—for there it was again. Cassandra calling out his name. *Screaming* out his name.

In an instant he crossed the room and tried to open the door of the spare room when, to his astonishment and fury, he discovered that it was locked.

Locked.

'Cassandra!' he thundered as he smashed his fist against the solid wood. 'For God's sake, will you open this door?'

But to his consternation he heard nothing but a helpless whimper from inside the room and, scarcely knowing what he was doing, he dashed downstairs to fetch the ornate brass coal scuttle which adorned the fireplace in the morning room. Scarcely noticing its weight, he ran back upstairs with it.

'Stand back!' he yelled. 'Stand well away from the door!' And he smashed the heavy scuttle hard against the panel.

It took him three attempts before he had splintered a hole big enough to be able to snake his hand through and unlock the door from the inside—and when he had snapped on the light he flinched at the sight which greeted him. Cassandra, all curled up in a foetal position, her eyes wide with terror as she looked up at him, her face deathly pale.

He was over to her in an instant, his hand touching her clammy cheek. 'What's happening?'

'I'm…bleeding.'

With a wrench of his heart, he looked down to see the crimson flowering on her fingertips and pain shafted through him. 'We need to get you to hospital.'

'I'm losing the baby!'

'We need to get you to hospital,' he repeated grimly and, picking her up, he began to carry her downstairs.

'Giancarlo—an ambulance,' she breathed.

'I can get you there quicker myself. Shh, Cassie. Shh. Don't cry, *cara mia*. Please don't cry.'

But Cassie could do nothing to prevent the tears which slid down her cold cheeks. She clung to him as he carried her out to the car, placing her inside it as carefully as if she had been made of porcelain.

A new sob erupted from her throat as he soothed her before climbing into the driving seat and setting out for the hospital and then everything became a blur of people asking her questions and her being wheeled into some sort of X-ray room where she was to wait for the radiographer to scan her.

And through it all she had that terrible aching feeling in her stomach and the sense of awful foreboding at what this was all going to mean.

'Hold onto me.' Giancarlo reached out his hand and she gripped it.

'I'm losing our baby,' she whispered.

He flinched. It was that little 'our' which cut him to the quick. The suggestion of togetherness which he didn't deserve—because he had been too much of an emotional coward to reach out for her. 'There will be more babies, Cassie.'

Brokenly, she shook her head. 'But not with you,' she whispered. She had offered him his freedom earlier because it had felt the right thing to do—never dreaming that he would be liberated by nature itself, rather than by the simpler act of her letting him go. 'Not with you.'

'No.' He knew what she was saying—for why would she ever consider trying to have another baby with a callous brute like him? And yet the realisation hit him like a juggernaut—leaving him feeling far worse than he could ever have imagined. A terrible pain tore at him as if someone had ripped his heart out with jagged fingernails. It was over. He and Cassandra were over. And mixed in with all this pain was the thought that his child had never had the chance to exist—and now never would. He remembered the online photos of the developing foetus he'd studied—and tried to picture at what stage his own little boy or girl would be at. But it hurt too much to try.

He looked at his wife. Her eyes were closed, her lashes like two feathery arcs brushing her snow-pale cheeks, and he brought his fisted hand to his lips and bit hard into the knuckles as if afraid that some primitive sound of sorrow might issue from his lips.

Yet he knew that there were words he had to say—and to say now, in case he never got another chance. He moved his hand from his lips and let it lie over her motionless fingers.

'But you'll find someone else some day,' he said unevenly. 'Some man who is worthy of you. Who can give you all the babies you want—and the love you deserve.'

Her eyelids fluttered open so that all he could see was the shimmer of wet violets—like dewy-fresh flowers which had been rained on.

'The love you never had for me,' she said brokenly.

Bizarrely, he thought of the Christmas wreath she'd made—the one which he had left on his door long after she'd gone back from Cornwall. He remembered the way she made him smile—the eagerness of her love-making and her sweet generosity. Not just generosity to him, but to his young niece—the child of the woman whose tongue had attempted to wound her. She had so many qualities, which he had simply taken for granted and had squandered—as if they weren't important.

He thought of the expensive clothes she had left behind and the coat in Paris she had proudly refused— and he couldn't think of another woman who would have done that. She had refused his initial offer of marriage, too. And at this, his mouth twisted. His *offer* of marriage—had he now reached new levels of self-delusion? There had been no *offer* of marriage—just a snarled demand that she fall in with his wishes, the way he expected everyone to fall in with his wishes, but especially women.

Yet there had been a chance even then for him to redeem himself and their relationship—but he had blown it. Even their honeymoon had been tarred by his cynicism—for he had subjected her to the inevitable hostility of a jealous woman. Why had he done that? Was it a deliberate sabotage? Some innate desire to try and hurt other people, as he had once been hurt himself? Yet the hurt he'd once felt as a twenty-one-year-old student was nothing compared to the terrible pain he was experiencing now.

Looking down at her lovely face, which still managed to be essentially innocent, he found himself swamped by the realisation of another, even greater truth. 'The love for you which I didn't acknowledge, not even to myself— at least, not until that night in Rome,' he said slowly. 'Because I convinced myself I couldn't feel any love for you—or for anyone. And that I didn't want to feel it. Because it brought with it pain—and bitterness.'

She shook her head—because this was hard enough to deal with without him heaping on extra layers of hurt and regret. She had tried hard enough to gloss over the truth—but now she needed to face up to it. Because she was losing her baby and she needed to be strong— not to indulge herself in the stuff of fantasies. 'I don't need you to sweet-talk me, Giancarlo—especially now. I'd rather have the truth—not some saccharine version of it. I don't want you telling me you love me just to try to make me feel better.'

'But it *is* the truth,' he vowed hoarsely. 'You asked me what I was saying to you in Italian that night I made love to you on our honeymoon. I was telling you that I loved you. I felt daunted by the thought of saying the words out loud and so I tried them in my native tongue to see how it felt.'

'No,' she whispered. 'You love Gabriella.'

He shook his head. 'I don't love Gabriella. Maybe I *did*—though it's so long ago that I can scarcely believe it happened,' he said savagely. 'But in many ways, she hurt my pride more than she hurt my heart.' He gave a bitter laugh. 'I've been a fool. A stupid, idiotic fool—and now it's too late. Because even your sweet and generous heart could never forgive me for what I have done and for what I have failed to do.'

She had never seen Giancarlo looking like this—with his face all ravaged with pain and his black eyes bleak with regret. And in spite of everything that had happened, she wanted to reach out and comfort him and cradle him in her arms and to take those dark feelings away from him. So which of them was the real fool?

'Giancarlo—'

'Mrs Vellutini?' A brisk voice interrupted her painful thoughts and a middle-aged woman with tired eyes and a white uniform walked into the room. 'Hello, I'm the radiographer—and I'm going to give you a scan. Let's try to see what's going on.'

At this, Cassie began to cry again—silent tears sliding down her cheeks as Giancarlo gripped her hand.

'Shh,' he soothed. 'Don't cry.'

'How can I *not* cry when I'm losing our baby?'

Never had he felt so powerless as the radiographer began to apply globs of clear jelly to the paddles on the machine and he stared helplessly into the white face of his wife.

And his own utter self-condemnation was followed by a rush of determination that she should know the truth. That somehow it was important that she heard it now—before their world was devastated by what they were about to discover. That there should be no misunderstanding whatsoever. No hiding behind a different language in case what he was about to say was flung back in his face.

'Cassie, I love you. I know you may not believe me and that it's all too late, but I do. I love you.'

Her eyes fluttered open and she stared at him, her pain even greater now—something which she hadn't thought possible. 'No, you don't love me. Please stop saying that.'

'I'm not going to stop saying it until you believe me. I've been everything a man shouldn't be. Thoughtless. Stubborn. Arrogant. Proud. Unable to acknowledge what was staring me in the face. That you make my world light up, Cassie,' he said simply. 'You've become the shining centre of it—and all the time I've been closing my eyes to it, and my heart.'

Cassie shook her head, unable to believe what was happening. Giancarlo saying such personal and loving things to her—and in front of the radiographer, too. Because he didn't *do* demonstrative. She remembered the way he'd railed at her in the shop in Paris for daring to jeopardise his reputation—but he didn't seem to care about his reputation at the moment.

'I don't know what to say,' she whispered, biting her lip with dread as she felt the cold dab of two paddles being applied to her abdomen—and quickly she turned her head away from the black and white blur of the TV monitor. 'I'm so scared.'

'Then say nothing—let me say it. Let me try and distract you from your fear, my love. Please, my darling— my brave darling. I love you, Cassie—and what I want is for you to carry on being my wife and for us to make more babies together. Only I know that I've probably blown it. That you have every right to tell me it's over— and to walk away. And if you do that, then I am going to miss you and ache for you—but I will accept it. I will let you go because I love you and I want what is best for you. I will give you your freedom, *cara mia*—if that's what you want.'

It was the selflessness in his statement which made her waver. The idea that Giancarlo wanted, not what *he* desired—but what was best for *her*. Through the shimmer of her tears she looked at him and drew a deep, shuddering breath. 'But I don't want my freedom.'

There was a pause. 'You don't?'

'Of course I don't! Why would I want to be free of the man I love?'

In the midst of their terrible grief, their eyes met as they sought to make some sense of their fractured world—as if wanting to bolster themselves with shared comfort— before they faced the pain which awaited them.

'I could have been a better husband,' he whispered.

'And I could have been a better wife.'

'And you will both be better parents if you stop all this soul-searching and have a look at this little heartbeat instead,' came the crisp interjection of the radiographer.

Giancarlo stilled. *'Scusi?'*

'Wh-what did you say?' stumbled Cassie.

The radiographer smiled as if she had suddenly discovered why getting out of bed at two o'clock on a cold winter night could be so worthwhile. 'Look,' she said gently. 'You see that throbbing little bit there? That's your baby's heart.'

Fingers of fire clutched Giancarlo's own heart. 'You mean—?'

'Your baby's alive, Mr Vellutini. Very much alive. Look, here are the little arms—can you see the tiny fingers? And the legs? Sturdy-looking legs they look too, from where I'm standing.'

'B-but...I bled,' protested Cassie shakily—and the eyes which had been unable to face looking at the scan now began to devour every bit of the screen for some kind of information about the life which—miraculously—was still growing inside her.

'It's not uncommon,' said the radiographer. 'It's nature's way of telling Mum to relax. Do you think you'll be able to do that in future, Mrs Vellutini—to relax?'

Scarcely able to believe how her world could turn from desolate dark to gleaming bright in the space of a heartbeat, Cassie looked up into Giancarlo's face. And a wide smile threatened to split her face in two. 'Oh, I think so,' she said, laughing.

'I will make sure of it,' he vowed softly. 'I will do

everything in my power to look after my wife.' And he lifted Cassie's fingertips to his lips.

'Then I'll leave you both alone for a moment,' said the radiographer diplomatically. 'Come out when you're ready.'

But they scarcely noticed the kindly woman leave, they were too overwhelmed by the gift they had been given—of the new life which still grew inside her and a tentative new love which would also flourish, if they let it.

'And we will let it,' vowed Giancarlo fiercely. 'Tell me how I can ever make it up to you, *mia cara* Cassie?'

She looked into his face and saw the tears which were glinting in the depths of his black eyes—surprised to see such a depth of emotion on the face of someone so essentially masculine as Giancarlo. But, in a way, being honest enough to show his feelings like that only made him seem more of a man, if that were possible.

'We won't ever dwell on the bad things which have happened in the past,' she whispered. 'Only all the good things—and those we will cherish and learn from.'

Learn from. Giancarlo nodded. Yes, he would learn. They would learn from each other.

Taking off his jacket, he looped it tenderly around his wife's shoulders and looked into her eyes. 'Home?' he questioned simply.

The sudden lump in her throat was so big that it would have been impossible for her to speak a whole sentence. Good thing, then, that there was only one word she needed to say.

'Home,' she agreed shakily.

EPILOGUE

'AND here. We put the last sprig of holly just...*so*. See? And just one more little tug of the scarlet ribbon—and our Christmas wreath is all ready to surprise Papa.'

'Surprise Papa! Surprise Papa!' squealed Chiara and clapped her little hands together. 'Papa loves Christmas!'

'So he does,' agreed Cassie, smiling down into her daughter's wide ebony eyes, which so reminded her of Giancarlo's. 'He *adores* Christmas.'

'But it wasn't always that way,' came a deep voice from the doorway, and in walked Giancarlo—flakes of snow melting on his raven hair as he scooped up his beloved four-year-old daughter and held her close. 'Papa used to hate Christmas.'

'Papa cold,' Chiara complained, but she snuggled into him all the same. 'Why did you hate Christmas?'

Over the ebony tumble of his daughter's curls, Giancarlo looked at Cassie across the room, his heart melting just like the snow as he studied her. Her hair was shorter these days, but she still wore it in a single plait if she was busy, and her figure was just as trim, in her low-cut jeans and emerald sweater. His eyes lingered on the sweater for a fraction of a beat longer than usual and then he slanted her a soft smile.

'Because I hadn't met your mother then,' he said softly. 'And I worked too hard to enjoy things like Christmas. And I needed her to show me all the things in life that were really important. Like the wreath she makes with you every year—and the mince-pies she bakes. And the way she builds sandcastles when we go to the seaside.' But more than that, he thought—and much more than Christmas—it was the warm and loving home which she had created for the three of them.

'How are you, *cara*?' questioned Cassie softly. 'Looking forward to the nativity play later?'

'I can't wait,' he murmured. 'To see my daughter dressed as an angel. I call that perfect type-casting. And do you know that the snow is coming down really heavily now?'

'Snow!' gurgled Chiara.

'I love snow,' said Cassie happily.

'Surprise, surprise,' he whispered as, still holding his daughter, he walked over to plant a kiss on his wife's lips.

Cassie breathed in the warm, earthy scent of him, thinking that life was so good it couldn't possibly get any better. But it did. It just kept getting better every day.

Following the scare of her bleed when she was pregnant with Chiara, she had spent the rest of her pregnancy resting so much that she had complained of feeling like a whale. And after the baby was born—and after much discussion—they had moved to a smaller house, which was more manageable. They still lived in Kensington— but Cassie had been adamant that she only wanted drop-in staff from then on. That the close-knit family unit she envisaged didn't involve live-in staff. But she worked out a way to ensure that everyone was happy—even Gina. Actually, especially Gina.

After Chiara was born, Cassandra and Giancarlo purchased a small farm in Umbria and installed Gina there to look after it—because she had confessed that she'd been longing to go back to her native Italy. The housekeeper quickly settled into the simple way of rural life—and it just so happened that she became very friendly with a widower who lived in the nearby village. Not only did they marry—but Gina also defied the odds by producing a healthy baby boy at the ripe old age of forty-four!

Cassie's mother had also moved into a new phase of life. She'd given up the ties and the isolation of running a B&B and had taken over her daughter's job in Patsy's shop. She'd added choir practice to her salsa classes and made new friends and, for the first time since her beloved husband had died, she really felt like part of the community again.

Raul and Gabriella had divorced—Raul had won custody and shed about eight years while his ex-wife quickly remarried. Her new husband was a cat-litter billionaire who lived in some style in Santa Barbara and, although Cassie sometimes worried that Allegra didn't get to see enough of her mother, she had her niece to stay as often as possible. And Chiara loved her big cousin. In fact, Allegra hoped to go to art school in London and she and her father were both coming to spend Christmas this year.

Cassie had learnt that of course Giancarlo's friends liked her. She just had to give them a chance to get to know her—and she needed to stop judging *them*. In fact,

Serafina was Chiara's godmother and she and Cassie had become good friends.

Even Gavin had grudgingly admitted that Giancarlo was 'totally right' for Cassie after all. He had left London after he'd inherited some money and gone back down to Cornwall, where he'd bought a surf-school. Last time they'd heard from him he'd been madly in love with a Californian blonde who he said made him think of milk and honey.

Cassie smiled. Life was pretty much perfect. In fact, she could think of only one thing which could possibly top her happiness…

She waited until after the nativity play, when the three of them had walked through the snowy, silent streets still humming 'Silent Night' beneath their breath. And Giancarlo went to put his daughter to bed and to read her a story while Cassie produced a pasta meal which she had learnt at her Italian cookery class. She was also learning the language—and she sighed. If only it were as easy to conjugate Italian verbs as it was to make a fresh pesto sauce!

She heard the sound of footsteps behind her and felt a pair of lips begin to nuzzle at her neck as she bent over the stove, and her heart speeded up as she turned round to wind her arms around her husband's neck.

Their marriage had—thus far—been pretty much perfect, too. Once Giancarlo had dared to let himself love, there had been no holding him back. These days honest communication flowed between them as well as mutual respect. And the passion which had always been there showed no sign of diminishing.

The only slight setback was their desire to add to their family. When Chiara reached the age of two, they decided to try for another baby, but it just hadn't happened. A visit to the doctor had assured Cassie that there was no reason why it shouldn't and they should just carry on hoping. But as time had gone on and no new baby had made an appearance they had decided to count their blessings and be grateful for what they had. After all, they had one beautiful little girl and knew how lucky they were.

But Giancarlo's expression was thoughtful as he lifted his lips from hers and moved her away from the stove.

'Something you want to tell me, *cara*?'

Cassie eyed him suspiciously. 'Like what?'

'Oh, I don't know. Why your eyes are shining so much more than usual. Why you keep biting your lip as if you want to tell me something but don't quite dare.' His eyes glinted. 'And why your breasts look so deliciously curvy these days.'

'Giancarlo!'

'Are you?' he questioned softly. 'Are you pregnant?'

'Yes. *Yes!* I wanted to wait until it was all confirmed— I've seen the doctor and she's as happy as a bee. Says that everything is just as it should be. But that's not all.' She drew a deep breath. 'There's something else. Something I can hardly believe. Darling, it's…it's…'

'It's *what*, Cassandra?' he demanded urgently.

'It runs in families—and it's happening to us. It's twins, Giancarlo—*twins*!'

'Twins?' His voice was dazed.

'Uh-huh!' She squealed as excitedly as her daughter but Giancarlo was silent for a moment.

He'd made a lot of mistakes in his own relationship with his brother, but at least now they had been properly reconciled. And he could teach his own children the importance of love and understanding. He could teach them well because he'd learnt from the finest teacher in the business. His beloved wife.

'Oh, *cara*,' he said softly as he stared down into her soft violet eyes. *'Te amo.'*

These days Cassie recognised the Italian words he'd whispered to her that night in Rome, when she'd felt so broken and confused—all warped by jealousy and insecurity. How liberating it was to be free of all those negative emotions—to be free to love Giancarlo as she had always longed to love him. 'I love you, too,' she whispered back. 'So much.'

Her head resting on his shoulder, their fingers entwined, they began to move around the kitchen—almost as if they were dancing.

And maybe they were.

There was no music playing but they didn't really need any—for they were guided by love and the slow, steady beat of their hearts.

WE'VE GOT TWO MORE BEAUTIFUL
ROMANCES TO ENJOY THIS CHRISTMAS FROM
SARAH MORGAN

THE TWELVE NIGHTS OF CHRISTMAS

Mills & Boon® Modern™

This Christmas wicked Rio Zacarelli cannot resist innocent chambermaid Evie Anderson! They have twelve nights of endless pleasure, but will it last once the decorations come down?

On sale 15th October 2010

DR ZINETTI'S SNOWKISSED BRIDE

Mills & Boon® Medical™

Meg thought heartbreaker Dr Dino Zinetti would never look twice at a scruffy tomboy like her—but she's got under Dino's skin! And this Christmas it looks like he'll receive his very own crash-course in love...

Enjoy double the romance! Part of a 2-in-1 with Lynne Marshall's

THE CHRISTMAS BABY BUMP

On sale 5th November 2010

Make sure you don't miss out on the most romantic stories of the season!

HIS CHRISTMAS VIRGIN
by Carole Mortimer

Jonas Buchanan steers clear of any woman who doesn't play by *his* rules… *Rule 1: he doesn't bed virgins. Rule 2: he doesn't do Christmas.* But Mary 'Mac' McGuire might well have Jonas breaking every rule in his book by Christmas Day!

FORBIDDEN OR FOR BEDDING?
by Julia James

Guy de Rochemont's name is a byword for power – and now his duty is to wed. But Alexa Harcourt is the one woman Guy wants – and the one woman whose reputation forbids him to take as his wife…

IN CHRISTOFIDES' KEEPING
by Abby Green

Pregnant by ruthless playboy Rico Christofides, Gypsy Butler is determined to spare her unborn baby her own neglectful childhood. But nothing will stop Rico from claiming his child… even if Gypsy craves her freedom!

THE SOCIALITE AND THE CATTLE KING
by Lindsay Armstrong

Socialite-turned-journalist Holly Harding is interviewing the infamous cattle king Brett Wyndham when their plane crashes! Forced to rely on Brett for protection, how long can prim and proper Holly deny their sizzling attraction…?

On sale from 5th November 2010
Don't miss out!

Available at WHSmith, Tesco, ASDA, Eason and all good bookshops
www.millsandboon.co.uk

2 FREE BOOKS
AND A SURPRISE GIFT

We would like to take this opportunity to thank you for reading this Mills & Boon® book by offering you the chance to take TWO more specially selected books from the Modern™ series absolutely FREE! We're also making this offer to introduce you to the benefits of the Mills & Boon® Book Club™—

- **FREE home delivery**
- **FREE gifts and competitions**
- **FREE monthly Newsletter**
- **Exclusive Mills & Boon Book Club offers**
- **Books available before they're in the shops**

Accepting these FREE books and gift places you under no obligation to buy, you may cancel at any time, even after receiving your free books. Simply complete your details below and return the entire page to the address below. You don't even need a stamp!

YES Please send me 2 free Modern books and a surprise gift. I understand that unless you hear from me, I will receive 4 superb new books every month for just £3.30 each, postage and packing free. I am under no obligation to purchase any books and may cancel my subscription at any time. The free books and gift will be mine to keep in any case.

Ms/Mrs/Miss/Mr _____ Initials _____

Surname _____

Address _____

_____ Postcode _____

E-mail _____

Send this whole page to: Mills & Boon Book Club, Free Book Offer, FREEPOST NAT 10298, Richmond, TW9 1BR